Winnie's
GREAT
WAR

Winnie's GREAT WAR

by Lindsay Mattick
and Josh Greenhut
Art by Sophie Blackall

Ⓛ Ⓑ

Little, Brown and Company
New York Boston

Text copyright © 2018 by Lindsay Mattick
Illustrations copyright © 2018 by Sophie Blackall

Historical images on pages 233–240 from the Colebourn Family Archive.
Page 236 (right): Photograph © David Rich. Page 238: Animal record card reprinted with permission of The Zoological Society of London. Page 241: Photograph © Michael Davidson.

Cover art copyright © 2018 by Sophie Blackall. Cover design by Nicole Brown.
Cover copyright © 2018 by Hachette Book Group, Inc.

Little, Brown and Company
Hachette Book Group
1290 Avenue of the Americas, New York, NY 10104
Visit us at LBYR.com

First Edition: September 2018

Little, Brown and Company is a division of Hachette Book Group, Inc.
The Little, Brown name and logo are trademarks of Hachette Book Group, Inc.

The publisher is not responsible for websites (or their content) that are not owned by the publisher.

Library of Congress Cataloging-in-Publication Data
Names: Mattick, Lindsay, author. | Greenhut, Josh, author. | Blackall, Sophie, illustrator.
Title: Winnie's great war / by Lindsay Mattick and Josh Greenhut ; illustrated by Sophie Blackall.
Description: First edition. | New York ; Boston : Little, Brown and Company, 2018. | Summary: "An imagining of the real journey undertaken by the extraordinary bear, from her early days in the Canadian forest to her travels with the Veterinary Corps across the country and overseas, all the way to the London Zoo, where she met Christopher Robin Milne and inspired the creation of Winnie-the-Pooh." —Provided by publisher.
Identifiers: LCCN 2018009916 | ISBN 9780316447126 (hardcover) | ISBN 9780316447102 (ebook) | ISBN 9780316447089 (library edition ebook)
Subjects: LCSH: Winnipeg (Bear)—Juvenile fiction. | CYAC: Winnipeg (Bear)—Fiction. | Bears—Fiction. | Voyages and travels—Fiction. | Winnie-the-Pooh (Fictitious character)—Fiction. | World war, 1914–1918—Fiction. | Canada—History—1914–1945—Fiction. | Great Britain—History—George V, 1910–1936—Fiction.
Classification: LCC PZ7.1.M38 Win 2018 | DDC [Fic]—dc23
LC record available at https://lccn.loc.gov/2018009916

ISBNs: 978-0-316-44712-6 (hardcover), 978-0-316-44710-2 (ebook)

Printed in the United States of America

LSC-C

10 9 8 7 6 5 4 3 2 1

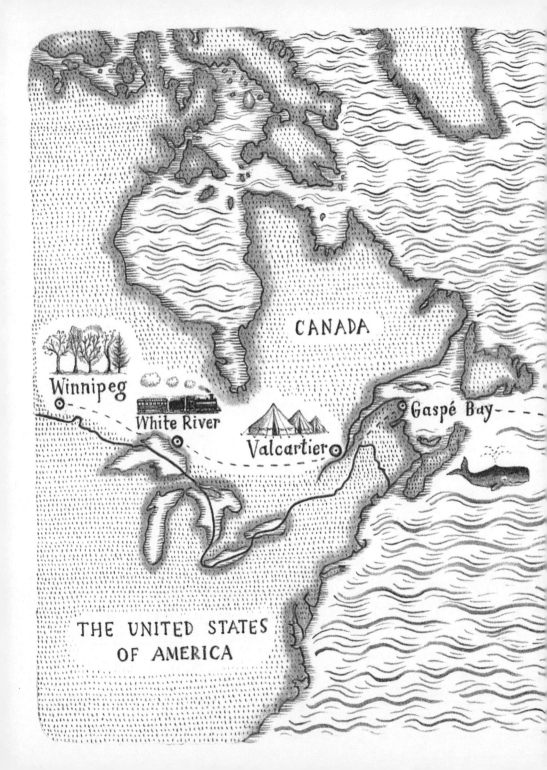

CANADA

Winnipeg

White River

Valcartier

Gaspé Bay

THE UNITED STATES
OF AMERICA

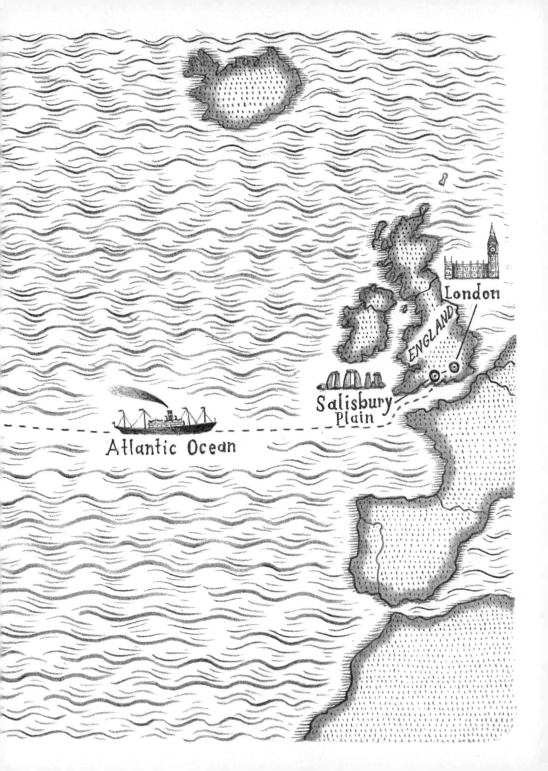

London

ENGLAND

Salisbury
Plain

Atlantic Ocean

"Do you want to hear the story of your Bear?" I asked Cole one night while sitting on his bed. It was already long past bedtime, but it was the weekend. In his arms, he held his old stuffed bear: floppy-limbed and faded, its fur rubbed to velvet, one eye reduced to some loose bits of thread.

Cole wrinkled his nose. "Can I have a story I don't know?" I could tell he was trying not to hurt my feelings.

I leaned back against the wall behind his bed. "Maybe I should tell you the real story."

"I know the real story. You've told me about my great-great-grandfather and the real Winnie-the-Pooh a million times."

"I never told you all of it," I said.

Cole did not look convinced. "Why not?"

"Because I didn't think you were ready." We looked at each other. "Are you ready?"

"Is it scary?" asked Cole.

I could not lie. "At times. But we can stop whenever you want."

Cole arranged his checked blanket around him, pulling its edge up to his Bear's chin.

"Proceed," he said in a serious way.

The Woods

In the middle of the Woods

was a tree, and at the bottom of the tree was a hole, and out of the hole poked a big black pad of a nose, which sniffed the air to see whether anyone was around. It smelled like a fine spring day, like the earth was growing.

Next came two great paws, followed by a pair of knowing eyes and a broad bushy back you could ride on. And just like that, a fully grown black bear stumped from her den under the tree.

After taking a moment to lumber around, Mama gave a wide yawn. "Come out, dear."

A tiny cub crept from the hollow. She perked her ears and raised her nose and spun round in wonder. "Our den is inside a *tree*?"

There she was: *your* Bear.

This was Bear's first time out-of-doors, though if she were like most bears, she would never know what a *doors* was.

Mama came over and licked her cub behind the ears. "Our den is inside a tree." She led her over to a different trunk. "Our tree is inside the Woods."

"The Woods smells like food!" The cub's nose pulled her about, over bumpy roots, along a rotting log, and up to a flower with a bright yellow scent, which she ate. She found some bitter green berries and ate them up and lapped water from a muddy puddle. She discovered a great mossy rock that she tried to climb, but she kept falling off. She gnawed at the bark of a tree.

Dizzy with the newness of it all, she returned to rest against Mama and her sweet, musky fur.

It was a very good place to think.

While the birds sang to one another about the wind, Mama groomed her cub by picking over the top of her head with her teeth. A question welled up inside your Bear. "Is anything bigger than the Woods?"

Mama's nose twitched and her belly shook. "I don't think so," she breathed, and her breath smelled of blackberries.

"What's the highest up any bear has ever gone?" wondered your Bear. This was later that spring, as she stood with Mama at the base of a white-trunked tree. She had only just learned to climb.

"Well," Mama admitted, "that's an unusual question." She scratched her nose with her paw and dropped her chin. "I've never climbed this tree."

Bear sneezed impatiently. "How high?"

Mama gave the tree a side rub. She stood right up against it and pushed her front legs straight and looked from one branch to another. "See that crooked limb way up there?" She pointed with her chin.

The cub's eyes searched. "No." And then, "Yes!"

Mama stretched her neck. "I'd say that is Higher Than Any Bear Has Ever Gone."

"I can do that!" decided Bear.

Mama lowered herself back to all fours. "You can, can you? You'd have to be very brave to climb that high."

So your Bear, she started to climb.

She climbed. And climbed.

She climbed and climbed.

She climbed and climbed and climbed.

She climbed and climbed

and climbed

and climbed

and climbed and climbed and climbed.

She climbed and climbed

and climbed and climbed

and climbed and climbed

and climbed.

She climbed. And climbed. And climbed. And climbed. And—

Her legs were beginning to ache when a gigantic black fly landed right on the tip of her nose.

"Please don't." Bear wiggled her snout. "I'm climbing Higher Than Any Bear Has Ever Gone."

Well, the fly had never been spoken to in quite the same way by another creature. He was touched. With a tiny buzz, he hovered aside. "Good luck!"

And on Bear rose through a cool, earthy patch of air.

With her legs wobbling, she rested her face against the white bark and gathered her strength.

And your Bear climbed. And she climbed and she climbed.

She grabbed hold of the limb and got her chin up onto it, and then one back paw, and then the other, and pulled herself into its crook. She shut her eyes and let her tongue hang all the way out of her mouth.

The Highest Any Bear Had Ever Gone!

Even then, that was the kind of bear your Bear was.

Her ears stood up. Mama's voice, distant and faint, sounded mad.

When Bear looked over the edge, she couldn't see Mama at all. It was a very, very, very long way down.

And all at once, all her hairs started to shake.

"HOW am I going to get DOWN?" she wailed.

Two squirrels came round to see what all the fuss was about: One was Fancy and the other was Tall. They scampered onto a high branch not far from the crooked limb.

"It's a bear!" marveled Tall. He sprung up tall and scrunched down and shot up and scrunched down. "How do you like that?!"

Fancy brushed back her ears. "I never would have thought that sort of racket could come from a bear," she observed with a toss of her head and a sweep of her tail. "Perhaps she's Himalayan."

Tall scratched his cheek. "Have you ever seen a bear this high up before?"

"Never." Fancy turned her nose up. "It's unnatural."

Mama's voice rose to Bear's ears. "Be brave!"

Tall bounced nervously. "I wonder why she's so upset."

"Hello!" Bear called.

Fancy and Tall froze.

"Haaaalllllllloooooo!" Your Bear had stopped whining completely.

Very slowly, so as not to attract any attention, Tall leaned closer to Fancy. "Is she *talking* to us?"

"Hold on," said Cole.

"Yes?"

"You said this was the real story."

"Yes."

"The true story."

"It is."

"Then why are there talking animals?"

This was a good question.

"Just because animals don't speak words," I said, pausing to consider my answer, "that doesn't mean they can't talk. Animals bark and roar and hiss and chirp at one another all the time. Usually, they can only understand animals like them. Cats understand cats. Whales understand whales. What made your Bear special was that she could communicate with just about anyone."

Cole squeezed the line of his Bear's mouth. "Hallo there," he said in a high voice.

Fancy and Tall could not believe it: a Talking Bear!

But while Fancy staggered backward, clutching her tail to her breast, Tall crept farther down the branch, studying the cub. He scampered back to Fancy. "She seems friendly."

Fancy glared at him with both sides of her face. "Have you lost your acorns?" Her tail pointed straight up. "It's a trap!"

"I know you see me," Bear was calling. "You! Yes, you! The gray things!"

With sudden resolve, Tall stepped past Fancy's tail. "We are Squirrels. How can we help?" Fancy tsked him loudly, but Tall went on. "We've never seen a bear this high up before!"

Fancy bit Tall on one of his hind legs. "STOP TALKING TO THE BEAR!"

Tall spun on her. "Why?"

Fancy whipped him in the head with her tail. "BE-CAUSE BEARS EAT SQUIRRELS!"

"Not always," Tall pointed out, with one tiny paw in the air.

Bear patted the crooked branch. "Do you know how I might get down?"

Fancy flicked her ears as if she'd had enough, and

with great impatience, she zipped over to a point higher up on the white trunk. "You just—climb down!" She pointed her nose to the ground, glided down until she was just out of Bear's reach, turned around, and raced back up.

"I see," Bear told herself. "Like that." She wiggled back to the trunk, slid her front paws toward the earth so she was upside down, and lost her footing at once. Frantically, she claw-clutched the white trunk, screeching.

"Not like that!" the squirrels chickered.

Mama's grunts floated up from below. "I'm coming! Here I come!"

"Silly bear!" Tall couldn't stop tittering. "Bears don't go headfirst!"

When Bear finally succeeded in climbing back into the branch's crook, she stuck out her nose at Fancy. "That's what she did!"

Tall shrugged with an air of apology. "We're Squirrels."

"We have bird bones," agreed Fancy, winding her tail.

Tall suddenly squeaked, "Big Bear!" The pair darted to a higher branch on the next tree over as Mama trudged up.

"This," Mama panted, "is very," Mama panted, "high."

The cub let Mama pull her down to rest in the place between Mama's neck and shoulder. Mama nipped Bear's leg gently. "Too high. You are very brave."

She began to climb down, leading Bear step-by-step.

By the time they dropped through the cool patch of air, Bear was wagging her head proudly. "The squirrels told me they'd never seen a bear so high up before."

Mama gulped as your Bear clambered past her on her way to the ground. "You were talking to squirrels?"

Curled against Mama's belly in the lightless warmth of their den, Bear noticed a thought trying to find a place to land, but it couldn't find a good spot, so she stopped nursing and asked, "Why were they scared of you?"

Mama stirred. "Who?"

"The squirrels."

"Because I am a bear, and they are squirrels."

"Oh, right." Bear went back to nursing, but the thought still would not stop fluttering about, so she turned over. "But why would squirrels be scared of bears?"

Mama licked her cub behind one ear. "Animals are scared of other animals."

"But why?" Bear pressed her.

"Because animals kill animals."

Bear put a paw to her mouth. It felt as if a tree were falling inside her chest. "No animals kill bears, though. Right?"

"The trapper does," Mama snorted. "Remember the trap?"

Bear's hairs stood on end. She and Mama had come

across the trap one day after a great rain. Its monstrous teeth were sunk into the neck of a dead fox. The scent of the trapper clung to everything.

Bear had not realized until just now that what happened to the fox could happen to her.

It grew darker and darker inside the cub's head until it was as dark as the den.

"Do bears kill?" she wondered. "Do you?"

"When I have to," admitted Mama. "When there is not enough food."

The cub wriggled around suddenly, twisting her body as if she were trying to get away. She scratched at Mama.

"We fight or we flee," huffed Mama. "This is what animals do."

"I didn't fight the squirrels!" yelped the cub. "They didn't run from me!"

Mama shrugged her great shoulders. "Then they must be very brave." She let her cub writhe and whine until, very gently, she placed her chin atop Bear's side to quiet her.

"Maybe I'm not like other animals," Bear huffed, wiping her nose with the back of one paw.

"Maybe you're not." Mama pulled your Bear closer. "But I'm happy you're you."

"You said nothing was bigger than the Woods!" Your Bear bounded into the lake as Mama trundled after her.

"This water is very large," Mama yawned. She ducked under the surface, looking for something fishy to eat.

Bear was in a wrestling mood. She charged up to Mama, nipped at her arm, and splashed out of reach. Mama grunted, "I'll get you!" and went after her. She caught her cub by the scruff of her neck and tossed her into the air, and when Bear crashed back into the water, she made friendly bubbles at all the tiny silver fish, but they darted away, so she turned back to Mama. "Again!" Bear begged. "Again!"

Afterward, they flattened themselves on a broad rock to dry, your Bear's limbs as heavy as stones.

The sun moved the shadows. With her muzzle resting on Mama's arm, the cub ran her eyes along the bright belt of trees that bordered the lake.

Something caught her attention: a string of white puffs marching above the treetops like baby clouds. New puffs rose to the front of the line as the ones in the back faded away.

The cub sat up. "Look." The puffs were coming round the lake as quickly as birds. Now she could hear them chugging like crickets.

Mama lifted her head.

"What is that?" Bear wondered.

Mama put her head back down. "It is too far away to harm us."

But your Bear wasn't afraid. She was curious.

Long after the puffs faded to blue, she watched the

sky. Thoughtfully, she nose-nudged Mama. "What's the farthest you have ever gone?"

Mama peered across the water. "To the other side of the lake."

"I want to go farther."

"How do you know it will be safe?" Mama asked.

There was a long, thoughtful silence, because Bear did not know.

She just kept staring at the horizon until Mama leaned over and scratched her on the back of her neck. "Only a bear brave enough to talk to a snake could go that far."

Bear's nose wriggled as if Mama had tickled it. Just that morning, Mama had found her deep in conversation with a snake! They had talked about which was better: legs or no legs.

Anyway, Bear liked that Mama had said that. She licked Mama's shoulder.

Mama leaned down and licked her head in return. "No matter where you go, you will always be my Bear."

Every day through the height of that summer, the cub and her Mama swam and climbed and ate and roamed and wrestled. Here was Mama, introducing her to the robin's raspberry bush, which had the sweetest berries in the entire Woods. Mama, hushing so Bear could hear what the snails had to say. Mama, snoring while Bear chased the crickets through the high yellow grass and then let the crickets chase her. Mama, looking up at the stars because Bear asked her to, and saying she had never noticed them before.

And every day Bear would climb a tree to watch the white puffs round the lake.

One day, when the berry bushes were almost picked clean and the green of the Woods had started to brown at its edges, Bear wandered off looking for a little something to eat. Mama had been napping by the lake, but when the cub returned, their rock was empty. She picked up Mama's scent by the shore and followed it in the direction of their den.

As your Bear crested a boulder, a piercing smell hit her: Mama but not Mama.

Mama in fear.

Bear crashed through the Woods. She tore through a thorny patch and between the roots of an upturned tree, the smell growing stronger and stronger.

Through a screen of leaves, she glimpsed the black of Mama's back in a clearing.

Mama was looking right at her. One of her front legs was held fast by a trap fixed to the ground by a chain.

The cub approached slowly and sniffed at Mama's ankle. When Bear licked blood, with its mineral taste, Mama winced and pushed her away with a long, low moan.

The wind shifted, and they both lifted their eyes.

Something was crackling through the Woods toward them, cracking branches as it came.

"Get up that tree!" Mama grunted. "Go!"

Bear bolted up a thick trunk at the edge of the clearing. Once hidden in the leafy branches, she looked down on Mama, who was tugging hard at the trap.

An animal came into view, its head hidden by a wide-brimmed hat.

The trapper. Fear wrung Bear so tightly she could not breathe.

But even then, she could not know what the trapper held in his hands.

She thought it was a branch. A broken stick, that's all.

Mama looked to where your Bear had climbed, then back at the man. She pawed the ground. She swung her head around and thrashed, the stake at the end of the trap's chain loosening from the dirt.

As the trapper raised the branch to his shoulder, Mama lifted her muzzle high. "Be brave, my Bear!"

"Mama!" Bear screamed.

And a terrible thunder cracked the Woods twice.

Even the insects hushed.

The trapper set down the rifle and removed his hat with one pale hand; with the other, he tugged his long white beard. Someone else, smaller, stepped into the clearing. The cub could tell by scent that it was a boy.

Shivering, your Bear tried to disappear, making herself small. She buried her face in the bark because she could not bear to see Mama's twisted body lying there in a heap.

When she felt the trapper and the boy staring up at her from the bottom of the tree, she tried desperately to stop crying, to keep quiet, to be brave—but she could not help herself. Not then.

The murmur of their voices seemed to shake the leaves all around her as they set about hauling Mama away.

The sun left pink streaks on the sky.

Up in the tree, the fly buzzed around Bear's head. It settled on the moist black tip of her nose, hoping to get swatted away. It poked into one nostril and then the other. But no matter how annoying it tried to make itself, Bear did not seem to notice or care.

Fancy and Tall stood watch nearby. Having wrapped herself in her tail, Fancy dabbed one eye with it. "Poor thing. A babe alone in the Woods. How will she survive?"

Tall's own tail had curved into something like a question mark. He hopped down beside the cub and patted his chest twice with one paw. "Your Mama was a great bear."

But Bear just lay there, blinking.

"*Be brave, my Bear*," her Mama had called.

Bear lifted her head and shook the fly gently away. Her friends the snails slid up the trunk toward her, and the crickets from the high grasses chirped kindly, and the red-breasted robin from the raspberry bush landed on the branch at her side and laid down a worm, who wiggled its respects as the loons sang out on the lake.

Your Bear was still in the tree when the boy came back shortly after sunrise the next morning. "Hello, Bear?" he called.

Bear put her paw in her mouth.

"Come down," called the boy. "I won't hurt you."

Your Bear wanted to growl, "Go away!" but she dared not make a sound.

"Please?" said the boy. He kicked the roots of the tree, and kneaded his cap in his hands, and paced back and forth.

He took a sack from his back and slung it to the

ground. His hands rustled around inside until he held up something wrapped in brown paper.

"Hungry?" the boy called, unwrapping it. The breeze carried a new scent up to Bear.

Her tummy grumbled. "Shhh!" she told it.

"It's chee-eese," the boy sang.

Bear squeezed her nose shut.

"I'll just leave it here," said the boy, carefully placing the food at the bottom of the tree. He searched the branches one more time before clomping off into the Woods.

Every day the boy came and left something to eat at the foot of the tree. The cub would watch him from a hiding place beneath a bush just outside the clearing. She would wait until after she was sure he was gone before tiptoeing over and scarfing down whatever he'd left.

A strip of chewy reddish bark that made Bear's tongue

itch: That was beef jerky. A bumpy brown thing with white insides: That was a potato. She took a tiny bite of a clammy white thing that was so awful Bear had to spend the rest of the day eating dirt: Oh, how your Bear hated onions!

Carrots. Moldy bread. A tin of beans she got her snout stuck in.

And then one morning something just dropped from the sky right at the base of the tree: a rotting fish skeleton. The boy's peppery smell was in the air, so she knew he was nearby, but he was nowhere to be seen.

"I want that!" her tummy rumbled. "Go get it!"

"No!" Bear told it. "It's not safe!"

"It's a dead fish!" her tummy grumbled. "What are you scared of? I thought you were brave!"

Bear's nose dragged her along the ground and up to the base of the tree. When she was just about to reach the skeleton, it gave a short hop out of reach.

Bear leapt back. The fish's missing eye stared at her innocently.

She waited. It did not move.

She prepared to pounce, and it leapt again! Now it slithered across the ground like a snake. Bear trotted after it until—

There was the boy on all fours. Around his finger was wound some fishing line, which he'd tied to the fish's tail. When she caught his eye, he looked down in a way that said, "I won't hurt you."

Bear sniffed again at the fish, and this time it didn't try to get away. When she licked it, the boy whispered, "I caught it myself."

Once she was done picking the skeleton clean, Bear sat and studied the boy. He had reddish speckles on his cheeks—freckles. Bear had a surprising urge to stick her face in the dark brown curly fur on the top of his head.

The boy sat back on his heels and reached behind him for a small jug. He pulled out the cork with his teeth and pushed the open jug across the bumpy earth toward Bear.

"Maple syrup," he said, and she could smell it. "From Uncle Owen's sugar bush."

The cub sniffed at the jug's opening. When she nudged it with her nose, it nearly tipped. When she did it again, it toppled. Bear rushed her paws out of the way as the golden liquid oozed across the ground. She touched the puddle with her nose, then cleaned her snout with a swipe of her tongue and—

YUM.

Bear's tongue went wild, stretching this way and that to get every drop. Soon she was a sticky ball of fur gathering pine needles from the floor of the Woods.

She sat up in a daze.

The boy started to laugh…and he laughed…and he laughed…and he laughed. "You look like a porcupine!" the boy said, laughing.

Suddenly she had a whole lot of energy! Crazily Bear raced back and forth and back and forth across the clearing. The boy whooped, cheering her on.

All at once, Bear collapsed on the ground, spent and happy.

The sun was high in the sky when the boy quietly rose and gathered his things. He slung his sack onto his shoulder, walked a few paces into the Woods, and turned, waiting.

"Come along," said the boy.

Bear blinked. She looked back to the tree, and back at the boy, and back to the tree once more. Feelings swirled inside her like leaves.

He beckoned with his hand. "Come."

And your Bear bounded after the boy.

As the boy marched through the Woods with the cub at his heels, he sang a marching song.

> *Some talk of Alexander,*
> *and some of Hercules,*

Of Hector and Lysander,
and such great names as these.
But of all the world's great heroes,
there's none that can compare
With a tow, row, row, row, row, row,
to the British Grenadiers!

The boy said, "Watch this!" and swung from a rope that hung from a bough over a dry streambed. The cub jumped after him, tumbling down.

Whenever Bear wandered off after some smell, the boy would say, "Come on, this way," and Bear would look up, her mouth full of leaves, and romp after him.

They were walking through a stand of pines when Fancy and Tall darted down one of the trunks. "What do you think you're doing?!" Tall screeched.

Your Bear pointed her nose after her new friend. "I'm going with him."

Fancy gagged, while Tall shot up tall. "You can't do that!"

"Why not?"

"He's not like you!" gulped Fancy.

Bear folded down one ear and pointed the other. "Neither are you."

"Baby bear," chickered Fancy, clutching her tail to her breast. "You will stop following that beast this instant!"

The cub pretended to dig in the dirt while the boy walked on ahead and the squirrels wrung their tiny paws.

"I heard you. You said it yourself." Bear licked the ground at Fancy's feet. "It's no good for a cub to be alone in the Woods."

"But he'll hurt you!" Tall pleaded.

"I don't think he will."

"How do you know?" Fancy tittered, twisting her tail. "You don't!"

Bear opened her mouth so they could smell her breath and then turned around to show them her back. "Try this." Her fur was still sticky with syrup her tongue couldn't reach.

Fancy stuck up her nose, but Tall touched Bear's fur lightly with one paw and sniffed it. He nodded with wide eyes at Fancy.

Hungrily the squirrels licked the last of the maple syrup off the cub.

"Tastes promising," Tall admitted. He lowered his tail. "We'll worry about you, you know."

Fancy looked at the cub with sudden tenderness. "We have never known a bear like you," she said. She stroked Bear's face with the puff of her tail. "You'll always be our Bear."

The pair scattered into the bushes as the boy came back.

"Silly bear," he said. "I thought I'd lost you. Were those your friends?"

The forest opened to an old cabin made half of wood and half of stone. A box of colorful-smelling flowers hung beneath one window. Gray smoke leaked from a stone chimney at one end of the roof, which was fuzzy with moss.

A barking black-and-white dog charged from behind the cabin. "Attack! Attack! Attack!" he barked. "Attack! Attack! Attack!"

"Sit, Leo!" said the boy.

The dog sat. "Do I have to?" he whined.

"Boy, is that you?" a gravelly voice called. "Come help! Maggie's ready!"

The boy threw down his sack and ran around back, leaving the cub face-to-face with Leo.

"Just remember," Leo growled, "who the top dog is around here."

"I will," promised Bear. She wriggled her nose. "Who is it again?"

Leo sneezed. "Me!"

"Right!" agreed Bear.

Begrudgingly, Leo wagged his tongue. "Good."

Bear waved her tongue back. "Good."

The dog carried on after the boy, with Bear rushing to keep up.

In a stall behind the cabin, a creamy white mare lay on her side. With every labored breath, her huge nostrils grew and shrank, grew and shrank. The cub sniffed at her mane, which was splayed across the hay-covered ground. "Are you sick?"

The mare lifted her head briefly, surprised at the presence of a bear cub. "No, little one," she answered, resting her head once more. "I'm well."

"Grab hold of the foal's leg," the gravelly voice said, and Bear took a startled step back. There was the trapper, crouched at the rear of the mare.

She almost ran away, but she could tell he wasn't trying to hurt the horse. So she just flattened herself behind Maggie's head and peeked over the mare's ears to watch.

Standing beside the man, the boy took hold of a bony leg sticking out of the mare's other end, dug his feet into the ground, leaned back, and pulled. Maggie's nostrils quivered. Leo lowered his belly to the ground, panting encouragement.

Patiently, the boy pulled a foal from Maggie. It came out wrapped in a milky blanket, which the man stretched aside.

"It's a girl!" said the boy. Maggie's eyes went soft and her nostrils released a gust of breath as a great happiness bounded across your Bear's heart.

The old trapper stood up with a groan and wiped his hands on a rag.

When he noticed your Bear, his white eyebrows drooped. "Is that the orphan cub we left in the tree?"

"Yes, sir," said the boy. "You said yourself that it was a shame to leave her like that."

"You know it's our job to trap these animals," the trapper said. "Not save them."

"I'll take care of her!" the boy said quickly. "I'll groom her and feed her and clean up after her."

"She's a bear, not a dog," said the trapper, tossing the rag into a bucket in the corner. Leo barked in agreement before looking at Bear in an apologetic way.

"Please, Granpa?" said the boy. "Just until she's big enough to take care of herself?"

The trapper tugged his beard. As he stalked out of the stall, he said, "Ask your Granma."

In no time at all, the boy was banging together a small wooden pen next to the chicken coop. He scattered hay on the ground and lifted Bear inside with him; he'd made it just big enough for the two of them. The boy, tickled by her claws as Bear climbed back and forth across his lap, giggled. Every time he pushed her off and rolled her onto her back, she rolled over and scampered back up for more. He went and got the old rag from the bucket so they could play tug-of-war.

Bear pulled and tugged and waggled her head with all her might.

"You won!" the boy cried as he let the rag go and she tumbled back end over end.

The boy ran to the cabin and came back with a saucer of milk. Bear hummed softly as she lapped it up while the boy brushed her back.

A high, shrill voice called, "Boy, where are you?! That bear better not be taking you away from your chores!" The boy nuzzled her and said, "See you soon," before climbing out of the pen.

A warm, sweet smell woke Bear from her nap the next day. She stood on her hind legs and peeked her nose out of her pen.

Leo, who was lounging nearby, sat up, wagging his tail. "What is it?"

The cub scratched at the wood that surrounded her. On her second try, she got halfway up the split-log wall. On her third, she made it all the way and tumbled over the top.

Leo's tail stiffened when she hit the ground. "Stay!" he barked.

Bear leaned her nose into the wind, trying to breathe in more of the scent. The clucking of the chickens quickened. "Oh dear!" they clucked. "Oh dear, oh dear, oh dear!"

The cub followed her nose around to the front of the cabin.

Leo ran after her. "Stop!" he barked. "Stop right there!"

If she seemed to be ignoring him, it was because she had other things on her mind, like her tummy.

"Stop! Stop! Stop!" Leo barked. "Stop! Right! Now!"

"Do you think it's blueberries?" wondered Bear.

Your Bear could see the open window, and smell something just inside the window, but she couldn't quite reach the window. So your Bear reached for the edge of the flower box and hoisted herself up.

CRAA-AACK.

The box crashed to the ground, scattering flowers in a heap of soil. Bear paused to eat them.

"Bad bear!" Leo barked desperately. "Bad bear! Very bad bear!"

Bear barely looked up. "These are good flowers."

After she'd eaten all the flowers, she dug her claws into the side of the cabin and climbed past where the box had hung. There, right before her eyes, was something round cooling on the sill. Deep purple filling peeped through dewdrop-shaped holes cut into a golden crust. The cub's lips quivered. "Oh my!"

She plunged her face into the gooey warmth, and the pie tin flipped off the sill and into the cabin.

Leo's barking got higher and faster. "Stop! Stop! Bad! Bad! Very bad bear!" Bear flung herself onto the cabin floor and ate the entire pie.

She looked around. Bear had never been inside a human den before.

The cabin had so many smells! Her claws clicked across the planks of the floor. She leapt onto a chair and marched over the table, leaving purple paw prints on a newspaper lying there. The headline read, CANADIAN TROOPS MOBILIZE—FIRST WAR SESSION IN CANADA IN A CENTURY.

The War had only just begun.

"What war was it?" interrupted Cole.

"The biggest, most terrible war the world had ever seen: the Great War."

"Who was it against?" asked Cole.

My mind raced all the way back to my tenth-grade history class, and my favorite teacher explaining all the complicated quarrels that led to the War. I told him, "Britain and Canada and their friends were fighting against Germany and its friends."

There was a speech I had to memorize. I put on a big voice and bumbled my way through it for Cole.

"In the awful dawn of the Greatest War the World Has Ever Known, in the hour when peril confronts us such as this Empire has not faced for a hundred years, all are agreed: we stand shoulder to shoulder with Britain! Not for love of battle, not for lust of conquest, not for greed of possessions, but for the cause of honor, to uphold liberty, to withstand forces that would convert the world into an armed camp; yea, in the very name of peace, we have entered into this War!"

I only messed up in a few places, I think.

"That's what the prime minister of Canada said at the session of Parliament they mentioned in the newspaper your Bear just trampled."

Soon Bear was prowling across the mantel over the hearth, and tickling her nose with a hairbrush, and kicking a tin of tobacco to the ground, where it made a terrible clatter, and chewing up a flavorful shoe. She climbed to a high-up shelf, which came loose from the wall, and all the bottles and jars and containers crashed to the floor, sending new smells into the air. The sunshine streaming through the window was hazy with spilt flour.

Your Bear was just licking up some honey from a shattered clay jar when the door to the cabin flew open.

It was Granma, along with Leo barking madly at her heels. When she saw what Bear had done, she gave a scream and grabbed a broom from behind the door. She came in swinging like the top of a wind-wracked tree.

Around and around she chased your Bear. The cub climbed higher, scrambling across a pair of snowshoes on the wall.

"Big trouble!" Leo barked. "You're in big, big trouble!"

"I know!" Bear whined, up near the ceiling.

The boy appeared at the door, carrying a bucket. He dropped it, spilling water across the threshold, and turned and ran away.

Granma was on a chair, batting her broom at your Bear, who was dangling by her front paws from a hanging oil lamp. The broom swept her bottom, and she tumbled through the air to land on the bed and bounce onto the floor.

The boy was back, holding a wooden crate. In a firm voice, he said, "Bear!"

Just like that, your Bear sat down on the floor of the cabin.

"Stay there," said the boy, creeping toward her. She stayed.

And the boy dropped the crate over her head.

The boy had cut a length of rope and looped one end around Bear's neck. Now she lay at his feet under the table as the family ate supper.

"You saw what she did, the little rat," Granma was saying. "Can you imagine the havoc she'll wreak when she's bigger?"

"She's not a rat," the boy said glumly.

"No, she's a bear!" shouted Granma.

"I promise," pleaded the boy. "I won't let her off the rope."

Your Bear sniffed at the boy's lap, wishing he'd share a little something.

"She has to go!" said Granma.

The trapper spoke up. "The cub'll never survive by herself in the Woods." His stockinged feet were planted flat on the floor.

"She's got a nice enough pelt on her," grumbled Granma.

"No," the boy said, banging his hands on the table over Bear's head. "She's not for fur! She's not for skinning! I saved her!"

"Watch the way you talk, boy," said the trapper, with a lift of his heels.

Silence pressed down through the table all around the cub. She rested her head against the boy's leg.

"Promise me, Granpa," said the boy. "You won't let anything happen to her. She's got no Mama. She deserves a chance."

Bear could hear the trapper taking a drink.

The boy was trembling. "I lost my Mama. Why didn't you get rid of me?"

Granma shifted in her chair.

"Enough," said the trapper in a hoarse voice. "I promise," he said, clearing his throat. "I'll find someone to take her."

Granma laughed coldly. "Who is going to want a bear?"

"Quiet now," snapped the trapper. "Finish your food, boy. That foal needs tending to."

August 23, 1914

Left Winnipeg 7 PM for Valcartier. On train overnight.

"Wait," said Cole. "What was that?"

"It's an entry someone made in their diary late that night."

"Who?"

"You'll see. Someone your Bear hasn't met yet."

At first light, Maggie the mare was hitched to the wagon for the trip into town. Leo, the boy, and the foal were all there to see your Bear off.

While Maggie bent her head to her foal, the boy knelt with Bear in the dirt. "Granpa's taking you to White River," he said. "He's not going to let anything bad happen to you. Right, Granpa?"

The trapper grunted as he climbed atop the front of the wagon.

The boy bowed his head, and Bear rooted around in his dark curls. When the boy lifted his face, she licked his freckles. They were surprisingly wet and salty.

"No matter what," the boy whispered, his face crumpling, "you'll always be my Bear."

He lifted the cub up to take her place beside the trapper and pulled the foal away from her mother.

"Sit down now, little bear," Maggie the mare gestured with her tail. "You don't want to fall off."

The boy and Leo chased after them, waving and barking. "Bye-bye, Bear! Bye! Bye-bye, bye!"

And that's how your Bear left the Woods.

White River

*A*fter a time, the trees turned to fields. The wagon passed one gray barn, then another, where a trio of cows lifted their heads.

She raised her mouth and they mooed at her, which made her very happy.

The houses grew closer together. Soon Maggie was pulling the wagon down a wide, dusty street under a steeple's shadow.

The man brought Maggie and the wagon to a stop in front of a low-slung building with a long sign over the door: HUDSON'S BAY COMPANY. He dragged the cub inside by her leash.

"I feel like I know that place," Cole interrupted.

"You do," I told him. "The Bay is where we bought your sister's striped pajamas. Nana Laureen got your white blanket with the green, red, yellow, and blue stripes from there. They used to have trading posts all over North America. That's how the department store started."

Inside the trading post, barrels of strange scents dotted the floor like stumps. Every wall was covered with shelves, and every shelf was full: dishes, soap, blankets, tools.

Bear eyed a tall pile of beaver furs in the corner.

"Surprised to see you here on a Monday, friend!" said a squat, jolly man with a furry face behind the counter. "You in town to see the boys headed off to fight at the station?"

The trapper shook his head and told him why he'd come.

"The mama's fur sold for a pretty penny, I'll tell you that," said the man. He stood on his toes and leaned over the counter so he could get a good look at the cub. "Why, she's barely big enough to be an out-house rug!"

Bear looked up at the trapper. "Don't look at me like that," the trapper said.

The clerk held up both hands. "I'm not judging, friend! How much you want for her?"

Bear rubbed her side against the trapper's leg, and his bushy white eyebrows rose and fell. He tugged his beard. "I promised," he grumbled to himself. "I did."

"And a promise is a promise!" said the clerk agreeably. "So how much?"

"Never you mind," the trapper sighed. "I'll see you Thursday as usual."

And without another word, he pulled your Bear back outside.

Whenever someone passed them on the street, the trapper said, "Cub for sale," in a half-hearted way.

A little girl stopped to play, but she was carried away crying because her mother was not about to buy her a bear.

Eventually, the trapper wandered to the train station, where he dropped with a groan onto a bench on the platform. Bear knew from the way he plucked at his beard that he did not know what he was going to do.

She heard the chugging before he did, and when she saw the tiny clouds rising in the distance, she began to strain against her rope. She was finally going to learn what made the fast white puffs!

As the locomotive came into view, Bear remembered Mama lifting her head from their drying rock: *"It's too far away to harm us."* But now here it came, barreling down, a Noisy Black Monster. By the time it pulled into the station with a shuddering sigh, Bear was hiding under the bench, rustling like a leaf.

Men poured from the train, flooding the platform with their loud voices and their big boots.

One pair of boots slowed as they went by, turned, and came back.

A soldier crouched down, peering at your Bear under the bench. He held out his hand.

He had pale, clear eyes and a dimple in his chin. On his wrist was a watch that went *tock...tock...tock* in the way of orderly raindrops, and he wore a dark green uniform buttoned high up over his necktie. He had a calming smell about him.

"Who do we have here?" he asked.

"Black bear," said the trapper. "I trapped the mama, and now I'm selling the cub."

The soldier felt your Bear's neck with his fingertips. He pulled apart her lips and looked at her teeth, and then he lifted her paws and traced their pads gently with his thumb.

"She's a healthy one." He gave her a good hard scratch at the base of her neck, which felt so nice her eyes crossed and her tongue dangled from her mouth.

"You want her?" said the trapper.

The soldier stopped scratching and got to his feet. "Sorry. The army's no place for a bear."

"I was in the army," the trapper said quickly. "Fought in the Boer War. That wasn't as big as this War's shaping up to be. Where are you from, Captain?"

"I'm just a Lieutenant. Lieutenant Harry Colebourn. From Winnipeg."

The trapper whistled. "Long way from here."

"Yes, sir. And we have only five thousand miles more to go. Well…," Harry said, looking down at your Bear. She stared back up into his pale, clear eyes, and something passed between them.

Harry faltered for a moment, as if distracted by a

lightning flash on a sunny day. He blinked. "I hope you find a good home for her," he said slowly.

Then he walked away.

Your Bear lay her head on her paws. She followed Harry's scent all the way down the platform, losing him, then picking him up again.

He seemed to be pacing back and forth.

Hold on—he was coming back, walking quickly.

Bear got to her feet.

"I'll give you twenty dollars for the Bear," Harry said breathlessly.

The trapper sputtered with surprise.

"That's my final offer!" Harry held out the bills, and the trapper gave him Bear's leash plus a hearty hand-shake in return.

"How much was twenty dollars back then?" Cole asked.

"A lot. Almost five hundred dollars."

"Was Harry rich?"

"Far from it."

"Why did he do it?"

"Why do you think he did it?"

"I think he wanted to save her," said Cole, balancing his Bear on his knee.

"God save the King!" the trapper called after them.

"God save the King!" Harry called back and looked down at your Bear, who was now bouncing along the platform beside him. "And we will save each other."

August 24, 1914

Left Pt. Arthur 7 AM. On train all day. Bought Bear $20.

"Boys," said Harry. "Meet our mascot."

A train car full of soldiers leaned in, looking down the aisle at your Bear.

A burly one with graying fur slapped Harry on the shoulder with his cap. "The Colonel isn't going to like this."

"This is the Veterinary Corps," said Harry. "Taking care of animals is our duty."

"I think that only means horses," said one with a playful smirk, pushing back his cap to reveal a swoop of slick dark fur.

The boys hushed all at once. A towering man with small eyes, hanging cheeks, and an enormous chin barged down the aisle. Harry saluted.

"Lieutenant!" barked the Colonel.

"Colonel Currie, sir!" said Harry.

The silence that followed was broken by a sudden lurch. The station began to slide across the windows.

"We are on a journey of thousands of miles," the Colonel's voice boomed at Harry, "heading into the thick of battle, and you propose to bring this Most Dangerous Creature?"

Your Bear looked up at the Colonel, who was looking down his nose at her, and she reared up with her mouth open to say hello. When the Colonel raised his hand to strike her, Harry yanked her down by her leash.

"She's an orphan, sir," Harry said, staring straight ahead.

The Colonel narrowed his eyes. "I'm not concerned with orphans, Lieutenant. I'm concerned with winning this War." He raised a thick gloved finger to Harry's nose. "If I have any notion that this pet of yours is any trouble at all, I shall do away with it myself. Do you understand?"

"Yes, sir."

"It belongs in the stable car," snapped the Colonel, continuing down the aisle.

"Yes, sir!"

Once the Colonel was gone, the boys all let out their breaths.

"I told you he wouldn't be happy," said the burly one.

Harry knelt down to massage your Bear's neck where he had wrenched it with the leash.

Someone asked, "What's its name?"

"It's a she," Harry explained. "I'm naming her Winnipeg, so we'll never be far from home. Winnie, for short."

Not until Winnie started chewing Harry's bootlace did they both realize how hungry she was. She'd had nothing to eat since the dish of cold porridge the trapper's grandson had fed her before dawn.

"What do bears eat?" wondered the boys.

"They're omnivores," Harry said. "She'll eat most anything."

"I have some vegetables from my sister's garden," the burly one said.

"That's very generous of you, Dixon," said Harry.

Dixon crouched before the cub with a brown paper sack. "How would you like a taste of Winnipeg, Winnipeg?" He fed her a knobby carrot and some fat green beans and a sunrise-colored tomato, which sprayed seeds onto his stiff green jacket when Winnie crushed it in her teeth.

He turned the paper sack upside down. "That's the last of food from home," said Dixon wistfully. "It's all rations from here on out."

Winnie puckered her lips. She was still hungry.

The soldier with the oiled fur and the sly smile came into the aisle. He held up something she knew: an egg.

Winnie reached for it, but he snatched it away. He passed one hand over the other, and now a second egg was there.

Winnie's eyes widened.

He waved his hand over the pair, and now there were three in his palm. Winnie blinked. He began to juggle the three eggs as Winnie's eyes chased them round. Soon she was balancing on her hind legs, swatting the air with her paws.

"Stop teasing her, Brodie," said Dixon.

"She likes it!" said Brodie, still juggling in the aisle as Winnie danced excitedly before him.

"Brodie," Harry warned.

Brodie caught the eggs in one hand. "Unlike some of you sore spots," he said with a wink, "this bear can take a yolk." And he fed her an egg at last.

Winnie was surprised to find the egg firm inside instead of bursting with ooze that ran down her chin.

This was her first hard-boiled egg.

She was just begging Brodie for another one when a stone-faced officer with a furry upper lip came and tapped Harry on the shoulder. "You'd better get her to the stable car before the Colonel comes back, Lieutenant," he said.

Brodie rolled his eyes. "Have you no heart, Edgett?" he pleaded. "We can't send Winnie to bed without dessert."

Dixon turned to Harry. "Do you think she'd like condensed milk?"

"I bet she would," said Harry.

"Not from our limited supplies, she won't," Edgett cut in.

A private a few seats away called, "Winnie can have the milk left over from my tea."

"Mine too," said another.

Dixon found a baby's bottle used for nursing foals and passed it around to collect milk donations.

"I'll take her in just a minute, Lieutenant," Harry told Edgett, scooping Winnie onto his lap.

He held the bottle to her lips, and the sweetness of the condensed milk swept your Bear away. As Harry fed her, Winnie's eyes drooped, and she began to hum.

Harry smiled proudly, and Brodie hummed along, and Dixon pretended to conduct her song with two pointer fingers waving in the air. Even Edgett's stony face let a smile peek through.

Row after row after row of boys in uniforms smiled down at your Bear as Harry led her to the rear of the train.

Each time they came to the end of a car, Harry lifted her into his arms and carried her across the roaring gap, over the pebbly tracks blurring below, before setting her down safely in the next car.

At last they came to a car without any windows, lit only by strips of sunlight that sparkled from between the slats of the walls. Winnie knew the smell of horses by now.

"Thirty-Fourth Fort Garry Horse, Atten-tion!" a moonlight-colored steed announced. The other horses shuffled their hooves, lined up as they were all down the car.

Harry laid his hand on the pale horse's muzzle. "At ease, Sir Reginald."

He led Winnie to an empty space where he looped her rope around a hook. "Mounts, this is Winnie," he announced. "She'll be sharing your quarters until we get to Valcartier."

"Yes, sir!" the horses nodded.

"Yes, sir," Winnie yawned.

It was very quiet, she thought, after Harry had gone. It was so quiet, it must be making everyone uncomfortable. Winnie wandered as far as her rope would allow into the middle of the car.

"Do you know Maggie?" she tried. "She's a horse too." Silence, except for the train on the tracks and the wind through the slats. One of her ears folded down. "She had a foal that came out of her bottom."

But not one of the mounts seemed to hear.

The train rumbled on.

All of a sudden, a great thunderclap startled Winnie. A storm-colored mare with a white bolt on her face had crashed her hooves against the floorboards. "What a disgrace!" exclaimed Tempest.

"What is?" wondered Winnie.

A towering black stallion with a shining coat nodded his heavy head. "Since when," Black Knight brooded, "do they allow badgers in the army?"

The rest of the mounts jostled.

Winnie rose up on her hind legs to show them. "I'm a Bear, not a badger!"

"Alarm!" A tawny horse named Victoria whinnied and reared in place. "Bear in the barracks!"

"Calm down, Victoria." Her sister, Alberta, tied beside her, was munching some oats. "She's no bigger than a feed bag."

"She could have big teeth!" Victoria fretted.

Bear opened her mouth to show how small her teeth were, but the car filled with neighs of panic.

"Keep your rumps about you, Mounts," commanded Sir Reginald at the end of the line. "I'll handle this." He swished his tail. "Are you friend or foe, Bear?"

"Friend!" answered Winnie.

"And you are prepared to fight for King and Country?"

"Fight?" Winnie's eyes grew big and round. "Who would I fight?"

"The Hun!" thundered Tempest.

"The Hun," stamped Black Knight.

"The Horrible Hun!" whinnied Victoria.

"They're not all horrible," Alberta pointed out, calmly tossing her mane. "Our mother was German."

Sir Reginald held his head high. "We are on our way to do battle in a Great War."

Winnie moved a piece of hay across the floor with her nose. "War?"

"War." Sir Reginald's head bobbed. "It is our duty to fight for what is right."

"War!" exploded Tempest. "When the heroes on our backs fire their guns into the hearts of the enemy!"

A hot, slow breath issued from the barrels of Black Knight's muzzle. "At last we shall have our glory."

Winnie's belly twisted inside her. She remembered Mama's lifeless body and the gun that shot her. Mama, whose breath Winnie could still smell if she breathed in deeply enough. Mama, who told her, *"Be brave, my Bear."*

Your Bear forced herself to meet Sir Reginald's eye. "I'm sorry. I'm not a fighting sort."

"Whoever heard of a bear that won't fight?" scoffed Tempest.

"The only thing worse than an enemy is a coward," fumed Black Knight.

Sir Reginald blinked solemnly. "Do you refuse to do your duty?"

Feeling weak, Winnie retreated to the space beneath her hook. She could feel the eyes of all the horses on her now.

Then she thought of Harry, and it was like finding the scent of something to eat when she was hungry. She moved back toward the middle of the car. "Does Harry fight?" she wanted to know.

Tempest forgot herself. "Lieutenant Colebourn? Of course not!"

A cool relief washed over your Bear.

"He cares for us horses," explained Alberta.

"He healed my leg." Black Knight raised one ankle tenderly. "That man has the touch, he does."

"He's the only one who knows how to calm my nerves," sighed Victoria.

Sir Reginald nodded his admiration. "Lieutenant Harry makes us feel better. That is his duty."

Winnie sat up tall and tapped the tip of her nose with her paw. "I'm like that."

Sir Reginald shook his mane like he did not understand.

"Instead of hurting others," she explained, "I make them feel better."

Sir Reginald studied your Bear. There was a long pause before he bowed his head as if bestowing something upon her. "Your duty is very important. May you always follow its call."

Valcartier

At dawn, Winnie was swept along with Harry and the rest of the Veterinary Corps in a tide of soldiers and horses that ran from the train station outside Quebec City all the way to the camp at Valcartier.

"We're a funny-looking bunch, aren't we?" Harry said, glancing down at your Bear on her leash.

"Who are you calling funny-looking?" Brodie said in a winking way.

It wasn't just that they had a bear: Every soldier wore something different, due to where they were from—some in stiff caps, and others in acorn-shaped helmets, some in green jackets, and others in red coats.

Edgett said they'd all be getting one uniform soon enough.

They came to a rise overlooking a field freshly sprouted with tents that looked like white flowers. Harry said, "Look at all the busy bees," and Winnie knew just what he meant. Men were swarming among the tents: digging holes and hauling wood, banging tools and shouting orders, moving and marching to and fro like busy, busy bees.

When they came to the dirt road that circled the camp, they stopped to let a marching column of soldiers go by who looked different from all the others Winnie had seen. The men wore floppy hats with balls like milkweed blossoms and kilts that swung about their bare knees. The peal of their bagpipes made Winnie whine.

Harry knelt and clamped his palms over her ears. "It's the Highlanders!" he announced over the din.

"Hey, Edgett!" yelled Brodie, pointing at the bagpiper. "Turns out you're not the only windbag in this army!"

Edgett glowered at him.

Inside the camp, Harry led Winnie and a handful of soldiers past men washing their faces in raised troughs, and stoking campfires, and sawing wood, and hammering boards, until they came to a group of tents with horses outside.

Harry tied Winnie's leash to a post before leading his men up to a sand-colored horse: Alberta, one of the tawny sisters Winnie had met on the train. While the men watched, Harry inspected Alberta's coat, and spread her lips to reveal her teeth, and lifted her hoof into his lap to look at her shoe. With every move he made, he spoke to the men. Then he gave an order, and they all spread out to inspect the rest of the horses.

All morning, Winnie watched how the other men listened when Harry spoke, and how sometimes he would watch one of them tending to a horse and then go over and show him how to do something. It reminded her of how Mama had taught her to climb, letting her struggle but then nudging her up.

The horses' eyes brightened whenever Harry whispered in their ears.

After the boys had set up a sick line for any mounts needing special attention—Winnie had watched curiously as they pounded posts into the ground a few bounds apart and connected them with rope—a loaf of bread and some dry sausage appeared, and the men plopped on the ground to eat. Harry kept rising to go talk to someone or do something, and the moment he came back, he'd be off again. Winnie sniffed around Edgett, hoping for a little something, but he shoved her back with his forearm, saying, "Masters eat first."

Luckily, Brodie snuck some sausage behind his back for her to find. Winnie rubbed her spine against his as she ate. Then Dixon waved a stick at her playfully, and soon he was holding either end while she eagerly held the middle in her teeth, and he laughed as he spun her around until her feet left the ground and your Bear felt what birds feel when they're flying.

After lunch, it was time for setting up tents. Each tent had one pole, a circle of canvas, and a series of ropes that had to be threaded through the canvas and pegged to the ground.

Harry, Edgett, Brodie, and Dixon tried setting up the

first one together. They said, "Pull it straight," "What are you doing?," "I know what I'm doing," "No, you don't," and other helpful remarks of that sort.

It wasn't long before the ropes were tangled and the canvas was bunched into a ball.

"Nice work, Dixon," said Brodie, tugging at the bundle. "You've got us tied in knots!"

"I'll tie you in a knot," Dixon growled, jerking the rope from Brodie's hands.

"You better not tear that," said Edgett. "That's army property."

"I'm sure we can figure this out," said Harry, scratching his head. "Let's start over."

It was Edgett who finally realized they were missing a rope and went to the supply tent to get it.

At last they got everything in order and tried to throw the canvas over top of the pole. It slid right off.

All of a sudden the world around Winnie cloaked itself in soft white folds glowing through with sunlight. Winnie hunted around, pushing the fabric with her nose, digging deeper, tracing one fold as it folded into the next. Outside, she could hear Harry asking a question, and then his voice grew sharper and his big boots were stomping around, while Winnie explored the winding burrow, getting loster and loster, until she poked her head out from under the canvas.

She could tell Harry was relieved by the way he suddenly slouched. "Oh, there you are," he said. "Silly bear."

In the flickering lamplight of his tent on that first night in Valcartier, Harry wrote briefly in his diary before crawling into his cot, exhausted. Winnie stretched on the floor beside him. His hand hung down to scratch that special hollow at the bottom of her neck that made her eyes droop, with his wristwatch tock-tocking in her ears.

"Some of the men are saying we'll win the War and be home by Christmas," he said. "You'll like Winnipeg, Winnie."

Your Bear yawned, thinking she felt at home already: It *was* a very nice den.

"I pray they're right," Harry said as he put out the light.

August 27, 1914

In Camp Valcartier. Orderly Officer of the Day.

Training began bright and early the next morning.

In front of their tent, Harry held an apple over Winnie's head. "Atten-tion!" he said.

Winnie raised herself straight up on her hind legs, with her eyes on the apple.

"Salute!" said Harry. He gently took one of Winnie's

paws and tapped it to her nose. Her feet staggered beneath her.

"Salute!" Harry said again.

She swatted herself in the face and knocked herself over. "Oops."

"Atten-tion!" said Harry again.

Sir Reginald came trotting up with Colonel Currie on his back. The steed nodded to Winnie in an official sort of way.

"Lieutenant Colebourn!" said the Colonel when Harry saluted. "What do you think you're doing?"

"Training our mascot, sir," answered Harry.

"Do you think training your mascot is more important than the training of our men?"

"No, sir," said Harry.

"I should say not. We have a great deal of work to do to turn this mob into a proper army."

"Yes, sir," said Harry.

"Since you are so good at taming wild animals, I am

appointing you Orderly Officer of the Day. As Orderly Officer, you are responsible for ensuring all the men of the Second Canadian Infantry Brigade are properly turned out. Every button will be buttoned, every salute shall be crisp. Should any man fail to perform his duties today in this camp, it is you who shall discipline him. You will see to it that all drills are properly carried out. If so much as a hair is out of place, I expect it to be corrected."

"Thank you, sir!" said Harry, standing even taller, and Winnie could see he was trying to keep his lips from grinning.

Once Sir Reginald had carried the Colonel away, Dixon's big, gray-furred head poked out of a nearby tent. "How about that?" he said. "Our Harry is Orderly Officer of the Day!"

The first bugle blew.

"All men at atten-tion!" shouted Harry, rousing the boys from their tents.

In the days that followed, Winnie went with Harry on his rounds. She strutted proudly beside him in her new uniform: Her collar fit smartly, and it had a musky smell, and the links of her leash tinkled in a pleasing way.

They never made it through camp without someone or another stopping them, saluting Lieutenant Colebourn, and saying, "Winnie, attention! Salute!"

She loved being in the army, your Bear. It was full of apples.

At the sick line, while Harry and the boys tended to their patients, Winnie took to wandering among the mounts. Some horses huffed or stamped threateningly when she approached—either because they didn't feel well or because she was a bear, she never could tell. But many grew used to her, blinking acceptingly when she came near.

Victoria appeared on the sick line one morning. "*Achoo!*" she sneezed. "Oh, help! I'm dying!"

Very slowly, so as not to alarm her, Winnie inched closer and closer until she was rubbing against Victoria's leg. She stayed still, just pressing her side gently against the horse, until the mare's nervousness settled. In time, Victoria lowered her muzzle and touched Winnie's head. "I feel a little better now, thank you."

One day Winnie went with Dixon to the depot where the horses milled about, and Dixon reached through the fence and held out an apple in his palm for Tempest, the moody gray mare with the white bolt on her nose. She crushed it in her flat teeth, and when a chunk fell from her mouth, Winnie hopped under the fence to get it.

"That's mine!" Tempest whinnied. But when she saw that Winnie was holding the piece up in her own teeth carefully for her to take back, the hotheaded horse cooled and reached her muzzle forward. They almost touched teeth. Winnie, close enough to see the creamy swirls that made up the bolt on Tempest's nose, thrilled at the moment of danger and trust they shared.

After that, even Tempest took to flicking her gray ears in greeting whenever she saw your Bear around camp. As for Black Knight, the midnight warhorse who had mistaken her for a badger, he continued to eye Winnie with suspicion.

It was Brodie who taught her to play hide-and-seek. He'd pass something under her nose, then run off while she stayed behind. When he returned, he'd untie her and say, "Go find it, Winnie!" She tracked a carrot to the bottom of a hole under a wheelbarrow. She discovered the mutton bone he'd deposited in Black Knight's saddlebag. ("Don't you dare," the stallion huffed when she tried to get close, but Brodie still gave Winnie her prize.) She even found the fish skin hidden in Edgett's cot—though only after tugging the sheets from the mattress and leaving dirty tracks all over his blankets.

Unlike Brodie, Edgett did not find that amusing. As punishment, Brodie was sentenced to one whole morning cleaning up after the horses with a soupspoon.

Three times a day, the men lined up outside the mess tent, which Winnie was not allowed into—"NOT EVER," Harry said in his serious voice, with a firm tug of her leash. The boys filed in on one side of the long tent and came out the other with their tin plates full. Wherever they could find a bit of space, they sprawled on the ground to eat.

Winnie was allowed to wander among them, sniffing hopefully. "Are you finished with that?" The kind ones always shared enough to keep her well fed.

But the smells from the tent called to your Bear without mercy. One suppertime, her nose and her tummy conspired against her. Before she knew what she was doing, she'd snuck under the canvas wall of the mess. The air was hot with scents: stewing meat, boiled vegetables, baking bread, milky tea. She tiptoed past a huge, steaming cauldron and stood on her hind legs beside a metal table, where she spied a block of butter almost as big as her head.

"Hey!" yelled the cook, and Winnie ran, her face all greasy with butter. He chased her out, cursing and shaking a very large ladle over his head. A second cook fired a potato at her.

She was just going back to find that potato when Harry snatched her up by the scruff of her neck, looking over his shoulder to make sure Colonel Currie wasn't around.

"I said not ever!" he said under his breath as he hurried her away in his arms.

"Oh, yes." Winnie nodded. "I remember now." And she breathed the scent of butter into his face because she knew it was nice to share.

The next morning a soldier ran among the tents shouting, "Currie is coming!" and all the men, including Harry, scurried around like squirrels, picking up things from the ground, racing in and out of their tents, and straightening their ties and hats.

A coughing motor announced itself as all the men stood at *Attention!* in front of their tents. She was surprised to see a strange wagon pulled by no horse sputtering toward them. It was the first time your Bear had ever seen a motorcar.

Harry shooed her inside their tent with not a very nice kick.

With her nose between the flaps, Winnie spied the motorcar's wheels roll to a stop. There were two men in the open coach. It was Colonel Currie in the backseat who stood now and looked down at Harry.

"Lieutenant Colebourn," he said. "I have heard disappointing news from the cook."

He hopped down from his high seat.

"Understand, Lieutenant, it is my responsibility to get this battalion into shape. I will not be distracted from that duty, and I will not allow my men to be distracted from theirs. I do not take the stealing of rations lightly. Did I or did I not tell you that if that bear of yours caused any trouble there would be consequences?"

"Yes, sir," said Harry.

"Where is the animal?" Colonel Currie said coldly. His gloved hand rested on the pistol at his hip.

Winnie could clearly smell Harry's sweat as he stood nose to nose with the Colonel.

When Harry did not answer, Dixon stepped forward. "Have mercy, sir," he said. "She's a very fine mascot."

"Even the horses like her, sir," said Brodie.

Edgett spoke up. "With respect, sir, losing Winnie would be very hard on morale."

"Silence!" commanded Colonel Currie. Pushing past Harry, he flung open the tent flap and stormed inside.

All the men craned their necks to watch as the Colonel tore apart Harry's tent. He kicked the chair over and slapped Harry's diary off the small table. He bent and peered under the cot before flipping it over and flinging its blankets into the air.

Then he looked straight up and went still. "Lieutenant Colebourn!" he called.

There was your Bear, scrunched up at the top of the tent's center pole, hiding in the peak of the roof.

"Come down, Winnie," Harry said, and she did as she was told.

The Colonel grimaced most grimly. "It is with no pleasure—"

Winnie rose on her hind legs and saluted.

Trained by habit, the Colonel's right hand rose from his holster to return her salute.

Then he realized he was saluting a bear cub. "Hmph!" He brought his arm back down and clasped both hands before him.

Colonel Currie and Winnie stared intensely at each other until the Colonel blinked. He leaned into Harry. "Consider this a warning," he said. "To you both."

"Yes, sir," Harry said.

A whistle of relief came from Dixon as the Colonel and his motorcar sputtered away.

"Did you see the look on Currie's face when Winnie saluted?" Brodie said with a laugh.

"Keep a closer eye on her from now on, Lieutenant," scolded Edgett.

But Harry's eyes hadn't left your Bear since the Colonel stood over her, and Winnie noticed that they seemed cloudy instead of clear. She thought he was angry, but then, with a bursting breath, he drew her close and hugged her tightly.

Because Harry thought of her as his Bear now too. She was just that sort of bear.

Once, only once, Harry walked her all the way to the far side of camp.

"What's wrong, girl?" Harry said when he noticed her dragging her paws and trying to lie down right where she was.

Edgett was with them. "Lieutenant," he said, "you must show her who's in charge." So Harry yanked her to her feet and continued on, though he kept looking down at her in a worried way.

All she wanted was to avoid the noise and the smoke. But they kept walking toward their source, and with every step, the blasts grew louder and the smell stung her eyes.

At last they reached the camp's edge. Quaking, Winnie peered out from between Harry's boots, and this is what she saw: an endless line of soldiers propped on their elbows, peering down the barrels of their rifles, shooting across a field—*Bang! Bang! Bang! Bang!*—as officers stood behind them shouting orders.

"A firing range three and a half miles long!" Edgett said with pride. "They say it's the largest in the British Empire."

Whimpering softly, Winnie cowered against Harry's leg. "I must get back to the horses," Harry told Edgett finally before letting her pull him back across camp, across the parade grounds, and into their tent, where she hid under his cot.

Harry got on the floor and put out his hand to reach her.

"It's all right, Winnie," he said in a gentle way. "You're safe. Nobody's going to hurt you."

Winnie turned away. For once, Harry didn't understand.

She wasn't worried about herself, your Bear. She was worried about him and the boys.

In the afternoons, the men sometimes played baseball using burlap sacks for bases. One day Harry and the boys were pitted against an undefeated team of Highlanders, who stood ready in the field with their bare hands on their kilted knees.

When it was Harry's turn at the plate, he carried his bat to Winnie and let her rub her back against it. "For good luck," he said, his pale eyes hopeful.

When he swung a few moments later, the ball went flying far off into left field, where two Highlanders ran into each other trying to catch it. Harry got all the way to second base.

After that, nearly all the boys wanted Winnie to rub their bats before they stepped up to the plate.

It was a fierce battle. The score seesawed back and

forth between the two teams, until the Highlanders ·
took a healthy lead late in the game.

In the ninth inning, the men of the Canadian Army
Veterinary Corps were losing by two runs. Harry was on
second base, Dixon was on first, and Brodie was up. He
held out his bat to your Bear and said, "I'm counting on
you, Winnie. Don't let me down."

With a fine line drive that shot underneath the short-
stop's kilt, Brodie slid into first, while Dixon made it
to second and Harry dove for third. Safe! They dusted
themselves off.

Edgett marched over to Winnie. He was one of the
only ones who hadn't come to see her yet. "I'm not superstitious," he told her, looking away while she rubbed
the bat and gave it an extra lick for good luck.

This was it. Bases loaded, bottom of the ninth, two outs.

As Edgett popped the ball into the air, Harry, Dixon,
and Brodie took off running. The ball shot over the center fielder's head, and as he spun and stumbled across
the ground to get it, Harry crossed home plate, followed

by Dixon. Brodie raced the ball as it sailed through the air to the catcher and—

They'd done it! They'd beaten the unbeatable Highlanders! Harry ran straight to Winnie and lifted her into the air, tossing her up and down, hooting and hollering as all the men piled around, reaching up to touch your Bear with the tips of their fingers.

There's nothing like a mascot to rally the troops.

One black night in Valcartier, Winnie awoke with a start. The ground beneath her was shaking, and men and horses were yelling in the distance.

Above her in his cot, Harry stirred. "What is it, Winnie?"

Then, as if bitten, he sat up. Together they dashed outside, and soldiers were running past them full tilt. "What's happening?" asked Harry.

"It's the horses," a soldier said breathlessly. "Some

drunken fool fired his rifle by the depot and now they're stampeding, thousands of 'em."

"Winnie!" Harry called after her. As fast as she could, she ran—your Bear, she could be as quick as a stag when she wanted—weaving among the ghostly tents, the strangled neighs of horses rising, her ears pushed flat against her head. She leapt over pegs and ropes. She came to the wooden fence around the depot and sprung to the top of a post.

As Harry ran up behind her, Winnie peered into the dust storm struck up by countless hooves, the haze broken only by brief glimpses of horse tails lashing in panic and the gruesome grimace of horses' teeth.

She spotted one moving differently: an upright white steed turning around in place with its head held high and steady as if to say, *Mounts, attention! Order! Order at once!*

It was Sir Reginald.

Harry put two fingers between his lips and pierced the chaos with a whistle. Sir Reginald was at the fence at once, and Harry climbed to the top rail and leapt onto his back. Your Bear wanted to go too, so she jumped, but Sir Reginald was already galloping away.

When Winnie landed in the dirt, a dark gelding reared over her, his front hooves churning the air, and they locked eyes—*Don't!* He barely missed her before galloping off with a shake of his head.

She bowed low as another shadow bore down, but now two big royal hooves were resting on either side of her, sheltering her from danger. Her nose rose to brush Sir Reginald's pale breast as Harry reached down, grabbed her by the scruff of her neck, and swung her up to ride in front of him.

"We have to stop them before they get to the river," Harry ordered.

"Yes, Lieutenant!" neighed Sir Reginald.

Sir Reginald strained at the bit in his mouth as they bored through the horses and bulleted to the front of the stampede.

Above the roar of hoofbeats, Winnie heard splashing, and the sheen of the river loomed. She brushed her chin against Sir Reginald's mane. "You have to turn now."

Harry strained at the reins.

Sir Reginald turned. And, because he was their leader, the tide of horses turned with him, slowly bending their path. "Turn!" Winnie told him. "Turn!"

Sir Reginald led the tide of horses in a wide circle, slowing them down in a spiral.

But still there were the unlucky ones. The ones who had led the charge.

Once the stampede was under control, Harry steered Sir Reginald back to the river. They trotted along the riverbank, Winnie's ears filling with the thrashing and screaming of drowning horses.

Harry leapt from Sir Reginald's back and charged into the water.

"Help!" he screamed. "Help!"

And there were Dixon and Brodie, rushing in after him, pulling a limp gray horse to shore.

They stooped over the mount on the reedy bank. Its long, clammy face was glazed with slime, and with a shock, Winnie recognized the bolt of white on its muzzle.

"Tempest?" Winnie's nose quivered.

Tempest coughed, and a trickle of water spilt from her mouth. Her eyes were slick and yellow.

Winnie felt a new presence over them as Black Knight stepped from the darkness. He and Sir Reginald stood gravely by as Harry and the boys tried to help their friend.

Tempest's breaths turned to rasps. Winnie lay down at her head.

Harry lay a gentle hand on Tempest's face, and her whole body shuddered as if a great wind blew through her, and she was gone.

Four horses including Tempest died in the stampede at Valcartier.

Winnie never knew the names of the others, but she always wished she did.

"Did horses die in real life?" asked Cole.

"Yes. There was a stampede in the middle of the night while Harry was at Valcartier, and horses drowned."

"They hadn't even gotten to the War yet."

"No. But it must have felt like war that night."

Three sunrises later, at one end of the camp's parade ground, Winnie stood with Brodie in the front row of men standing at attention. Everyone was facing the raised wooden platform where Harry now stood before Colonel Currie.

Sir Reginald, who was stationed beside the platform while the Colonel did his duty, nodded solemnly at your Bear. The other mounts—Black Knight, Alberta, Victoria, and the rest—watched with soldiers astride their backs.

Winnie stood very still as Colonel Currie pinned a third golden diamond on Harry's shoulder above the two that were already there.

"Lieutenant Colebourn," said the Colonel. "For your service and in recognition of your leadership in the field, you are promoted to the rank of Captain."

Harry saluted, and then all the men did. Winnie did too.

When the ceremony was over and the Colonel said, "Dismissed," Brodie, Edgett, and Dixon gathered around Harry to shake his hand.

"I never thought you'd make Captain before me," said Edgett.

"Me neither," admitted Harry.

That day Harry led the men in their drills, with Winnie marching alongside the rows of their boots, her head held high, her steps stretching to match their strides, the legs of the Second Canadian Infantry Brigade swinging as one, just like the legs of a centipede.

Your Bear suspected something because the men had been buzzing even more busily than usual. Brodie, Edgett, and Dixon had folded up all the tarps and packed all the veterinary supplies into trunks. Motorcars and horse-drawn wagons, loaded up so high they looked like moving mountains, were driven away from camp.

There was a different smell about the men. They were excited.

At night, after writing in his diary, Harry lay staring at the ceiling with Winnie on the floor. The tent had nothing in it now but Harry, the cub, and the cot.

A terrible thought bounded into Winnie's head: *Is Harry going away?*

Harry must have heard her thinking, because he said her name and pulled her onto his chest.

"We're shipping out tomorrow," he said with some sadness. "I understand if you don't want to go, Winnie. It's not fair to take you so far away. But—"

Winnie thumped him with her paw and touched her nose to his dimple.

Harry tucked in his chin. "Not many bears have crossed the Atlantic Ocean before," he said, raising one eyebrow. "You could be the first."

Winnie stood right up on his chest and licked his face.

Your Bear was always ready for an adventure.

The Atlantic

September 29, 1914

Anchored in the Bay with other liners.

*F*rom high on one mast of
the SS *Manitou*, your Bear looked out. Other boats
were arranged across the bay, dotting the water as far as
she could see. *This water is even bigger than the lake!*
she thought.

"Winnie!" called Harry.

She clambered down and he leashed her up. "Don't
go up there," he said.

Dixon gave Winnie's flank a good rubbing, and she sat on his boot so he'd keep it up. "We'll be on our way any second now, Winnipeg," he told her.

September 30, 1914
Same as Tues., anchored Gas Bay.

"Harry wrote Gas Bay in his diary, but the place's real name is Gaspé. With a p. It's French," I said.
"Gas Bay is better," said Cole.
"Totally."

Winnie liked life on the SS *Manitou*. She liked to play games on deck, and climb up and down ladders, and wander the narrow corridors where the cabins were. As far as she knew, they'd probably reach the other side of the ocean any moment now, so she'd better make the most of it.

A stone skittered across the deck to Dixon, who kicked it back to Brodie, who kicked it to Harry, who kicked it to—

Winnie bounded between their legs, grabbed the stone in her mouth, and ran up one of the masts.

"Winnie, no!" the boys yelled.

She came down and dropped the stone on Dixon's foot. "Ow!" he cried before angrily throwing it over the railing. The boys groaned as the rock dove like a pelican into the waves.

Dixon removed his hat and ran his thick fingers through his graying fur. "Aren't we leaving yet?"

October 1, 1914
Same as Wed., anchored Gas Bay.

Dixon shoved himself off the ship's railing and spun around. "What are we waiting for?" he barked.

Winnie sat raptly in front of Brodie, who was sitting against the railing with his knees up, shuffling cards in fanciful ways. "Dixon's right, Captain," he said. "We haven't moved an inch."

Harry looked up from where he stood double-checking the list of horses, Edgett at his side. His pale eyes squinted in the sun. "You try loading thirty thousand men and seventy-five hundred horses onto boats and getting them all in line," he said. "See how long it takes you."

Edgett narrowed his face like a hawk spotting its prey. "Is there something you're not telling us, Captain Cole-bourn?"

The dimple in Harry's chin twitched, and he looked at his hands. "You're right. You deserve to know."

"Know what?"

"There have been reports of German submarines," Harry said. "They're holding us here until it's safe."

Winnie felt a wave of dread drench the boys.

But a short time later, Dixon cried, "Look!"

Winnie stood with her front paws on the railing. Dixon was pointing across the water at the next ship over, which had a giant chain being raised into its hull.

Now she felt a quaking below.

"Anchors aweigh!" cried Brodie.

Within moments, the deck was so overcrowded with men that Harry lifted Winnie into his arms so she could see.

All together, the ships began slipping swiftly along, etching shapes like white gulls on the surface of the water. Your Bear leaned into the breeze to drink the salty wind.

At last they were really crossing the ocean!

How much bigger than the lake can it be? wondered your Bear.

When the waters reared and bucked like a mount trying to toss its rider, Winnie raced from one end of the deck to the other, plunging through the waves that crashed over the railing. With glee, she shot past one staggering man after another.

She spotted Harry rushing below deck, so she followed. He was bent nearly double, feeling his way along one wall of the narrow hall to their cabin.

When she caught up with him, his eyes watered at her in a pleading way. His face was as pale as Sir Reginald's.

"You're not well," Winnie could tell.

The ship keeled. With a helpless look, Harry pressed his lips together and rattled the cabin's door until finally it opened and he dove for the tin chamber pot and missed and threw up all over the floor.

In the ship's hospital, your Bear made her rounds.

The room was packed tightly with bunk beds, and every one of them held a seasick man. A sharp odor tickled her nose.

Winnie went from bed to bed, attending to each patient with a sniff of their blankets and letting them pet her if they wanted.

Once she made her rounds, she returned to the corner farthest from the door, paused to rub her side against Brodie sleeping in the bottom bunk, and climbed up to where Harry lay miserably. He was shivering, so she curled up with her back pressed into his belly to warm him.

The ship lurched, and ugly sounds spurted from throats throughout the hospital room.

A new man in a white smock and spectacles came to check on Harry. When he saw your Bear, he said, "What is— Shoo! Out of here!" and swatted at her with his clipboard.

"Let her stay," said Harry. "She's our mascot."

"She could be the King of England," said the doctor. "Absolutely no animals in hospital!"

"Are you calling the King of England an animal?" Brodie cracked from the bottom bunk, earning a few weak chuckles from the other patients.

The last thing your Bear saw was Harry sitting up, watching helplessly as the doctor chased her out the door.

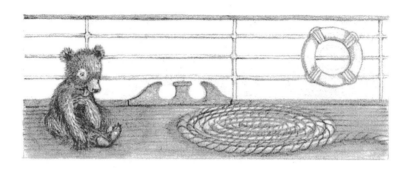

October 7, 1914

In hospital.

At dusk on deck Winnie took a break from her puddle-splashing to lick the sea's saltiness from her fur. Seeing a light glowing from inside the control tower, she went to prowl its window ledge.

Two officers were inside, one tall, one short, their faces lit by a lantern. When the short one noticed

Winnie, his muffled shout sounded through the glass. The tall one leaned forward and banged the window with his fist. *Bang! Bang! Bang!*

She lifted her paw and tapped the glass back. *Thwap! Thwap! Thwap!*

She always liked playing games, your Bear.

The man banged harder. *Bang! Bang! Bang! Bang!*

Winnie countered. *Thwap! Thwap! Thwap! Thwap!*

But neither of the men looked amused. In fact, the short one grabbed a long hook from beside the door and rushed outside to meet her.

Game or not, Winnie knew by now that it was a good idea to stay clear of angry people waving things over their heads.

She fled from the shouting men, bounding across the deck and diving through an open hatch, scrambling down one ladder and then another, racing along a curved wall, shooting through a portal, and skittering around a corner—

Winnie stopped with upright ears and nose alert;

she couldn't hear the men's voices or smell them any longer.

She stretched her front and back paws and started exploring. She'd never been to this part of the ship before.

The walls had given way to angles of bolted metal. Fat pipes and square ducts crossed overhead.

Still drenched from outside, Winnie shook herself, and the drops that flew from her fur hissed against hot metal. Down a corridor of machinery, some men with their sleeves rolled up above their elbows were shoveling coal from wheelbarrows into small metal doors. The fire inside was blazing so hot that Winnie could feel it from where she stood.

Something rustled nearby. "Hey!" a tiny voice called.

Winnie's eyes searched. The men shoveling coal hadn't looked up from their work. There appeared to be no one else around.

"Hey, you!" squeaked Whatever-It-Was. Winnie glimpsed something small and black flit past where a pipe dropped through the floor.

"Who's that?" Winnie had known many animals, but not one other than Harry had ever spoken to her first.

"Tatters is my name!" A small rodent darted right up to Winnie's paws and gazed up at her with bugging eyes. His fur was exactly the same color as hers.

"I'm Winnie."

"I didn't know rats could be as big as you!" squeaked Tatters.

Winnie was about to point out that she was a bear when Tatters asked, "How old do you have to be to get that big?"

"I don't *think* I'm old."

Tatters ran up Winnie's side and poked his nose in her ear. "When were you born?" he asked.

Somehow it already seemed too late for Winnie to mention that she wasn't a rat.

But what does it matter if we're different? your Bear thought. *Why should that stand between us?*

"I was born in winter," said Winnie, remembering the warmth of the den in the Woods.

"Winter!" Tatters squeaked, slipping back down and running in a circle around her. "That's almost all the seasons ago! You're an old lady! I'm only three moons old!" He scratched one ear with a hind leg. "You remind me of my cousin Bobo. She was plumpish."

"Is she here too?"

"No." Tatters's whiskers wavered. "She got killed."

"She did?" Winnie blinked. "My Mama got killed."

Both of them silently chewed something inside their cheeks.

The small rat's tail swiped the floor in a changing-the-subject sort of way. He looked sideways at Winnie. "Hungry?"

Winnie's tummy answered, "Always!"

They had a lot in common, those two.

Down the corridor, two of the men looked up suddenly as if they'd heard something.

"Let's go!" squeaked Tatters. And together they climbed up the pipe.

October 8, 1914
In hospital.

Scurrying in the gaps between walls and squeezing beneath floors, Tatters showed your Bear all the ship's finest spots: Salted Cod Corner. The Valley of Fallen Peas. Crumb Alley. The Bin of Sticky Tins. Leaky Faucet Falls. Rubbish Row.

Now Tatters led the way down a wall.

"Do you smell that?" His tail wriggled.

"I sure do." They crawled under the webbed shadow of an empty hammock.

Tatters sniffed. "I think there's something in here." Delicately, he chewed through one corner of a soldier's canvas kit bag.

Winnie nudged her new friend aside and tore the whole thing open with her claws.

"Nice work," Tatters remarked.

They picked through the contents until they discovered a large chocolate bar, which they shared.

Shortly after, Winnie got a terrible tummy ache.

"Because she ate too much?" asked Cole.

"No, because she ate that chocolate bar. Bears can't eat chocolate. It makes them sick."

"Really?" said Cole, annoyed. He looked at his Bear. "No more Halloween candy for you."

Tatters took Winnie to his nest, a mess of straw, cloth scraps, and paper shreds at the back of a storeroom shelf. There, he rubbed the softest part of his ears against Winnie's belly until she fell asleep.

When your Bear woke up the next morning, she felt much better.

Tatters held a crust of bread out to her doubtfully. "Hungry?"

"A little." Winnie pushed forward her lips and took it in her mouth.

After that, your Bear and the little black rat were inseparable.

October 9, 1914
In hospital.

They were grooming each other in Tatters's nest.

"Nobody's done that for me since my Mama." Winnie wriggled cozily as Tatters carefully picked through the fur behind your Bear's ears.

"How did she die?" asked Tatters.

Winnie remembered that day in the Woods: the

fur-chilling fear, the look in Mama's eyes, the thundering shots from the rifle. *Be brave, my Bear!* "She got caught in a trap."

Tatters scratched the base of Winnie's neck in an understanding way. Rats know about traps.

When it was time to switch, Tatters dropped down to sit between Winnie's paws.

"What happened to your cousin?" Winnie wondered.

Tatters shivered a little at the thought. "Bobo was looking for food in the hold where the horses travel. And a mad hoof flattened her."

"What an awful accident!" sniffled Winnie in an understanding way.

"What?" Tatters spun around. "Horses are monsters! Every rat knows that. They'd just as soon crush your skull as look at you."

"Some horses are nice," suggested Winnie, thinking of Maggie and Sir Reginald and the other good horses she knew.

Tatters's eyes flashed red. "Horses are evil!" he squealed. "They murdered my cousin and countless more!"

Shaken, Winnie backed away.

"*Animals kill animals*," Mama had told her. It was how animals were.

It took a long time before Tatters calmed down enough to let your Bear finish grooming him.

October 10, 1914
In hospital.

"Let's have something special for supper," suggested Tatters.

"Okay!" Winnie waddled after her friend's swinging

tail. They jumped up and walked across a chain that hung high over the men shoveling coal.

This would have been their seventh supper that evening.

"Where are we going?" Winnie wanted to know.

"Bobo always said if you're looking for a feast, find the leader of the pack." Tatters slipped through a jagged hole where the wall had rusted through. Winnie tried to follow, but it was hard to fit more than her nose. She pulled with her front paws, and pushed with her back paws, and then her ears were on the other side, and then her shoulders, and then—

"I'm too big!" Winnie squirmed. She couldn't go on and she couldn't go back! Her view of the room was blocked by a heavy chest—all she could make out was the back leg of a wooden chair, but she could smell the hot food on the table and hear the clanking of forks on dishes.

"You're too big!" agreed Tatters. He slipped back to the other side of the wall, and Winnie felt his tiny paws at her side. Frantically the rat scratched at the rusted edge around Winnie's middle, hoping to loosen its hold.

Winnie held her breath. The men were talking.

"Yes, we saved Paris, but a quarter of a million Allied men paid the price."

She recognized that voice!

"Shhhhhhhh! Do you hear that?"

"What?"

"That scratching."

Winnie began to shake, listening to the men listening.

The chair leg scraped back abruptly. Big boots thudded toward the trunk as the wall by her armpit crumbled and Tatters poked his head through.

"I did it!" squeaked Tatters, but his eyes bugged and his face froze as a shadow fell over them.

Colonel Currie shrieked and jumped into the air at the unexpected sight of your Bear.

The Colonel was not a man who liked surprises. "Major!" he shouted, instantly regaining control of himself.

An officer who smelled like onions appeared behind the Colonel. Winnie hated onions.

"Where is Captain Colebourn?" Colonel Currie demanded.

"He's been in hospital for the last three days, sir," said Major Onions.

"Well," said the Colonel. "Take this animal down to the cargo hold where it belongs!"

Major Onions yanked Winnie out by her front legs, scraping her side. As he hauled her away, she twisted around, partly to get her nose away from his stench and partly to look back at the hole in the wall.

Your Bear was happy Tatters had escaped. But she was sorry to see him go.

October 11, 1914

In hospital.

Winnie wriggled as Major Onions stomped along with his fist clamped around her neck. Opening a trapdoor with his free hand, he barged down a ramp. He flung your Bear to the floor and leaned down to chain her up, breathing onion gas right into her face.

"Ewwww!" she howled.

When he slammed the trapdoor behind him, darkness swallowed the hold.

Hooves shuffled. "Winnie, is that you?"

She turned, tripping over the chain that held her. "Sir Reginald?" All around her, the ghostly forms of horses moved.

"Winnie," Sir Reginald huffed. "Where is Captain Colebourn?"

"He's sick," she told them. "The sea doesn't agree with him. Food keeps coming up from his tummy."

"If only it was that easy for horses," said Alberta sadly.

Victoria made a pitiful noise, and Winnie knew that she was in pain.

"We need help, Winnie," Sir Reginald said. "We have been poisoned."

"Poisoned?"

Black Knight shuddered. "Poisoned by *rats*."

"Rats?" Winnie sniffed the air carefully.

"They put filth in our feed," Sir Reginald told her.

Sure enough, Winnie smelled Tatters nearby.

There was a faint, questioning squeak. Tiny steps pattered closer, stopped, came closer still.

"They have us surrounded," Sir Reginald told Winnie.

"Let them come." Black Knight shook his mane. "And I will crush every one."

Winnie focused on a point in the darkness.

"Winnie!" Tatters's nose poked from the shadows and sniffed at Winnie's chain. "The horses are holding you prisoner!"

"No, they're not." Winnie shook her head. "They're my friends."

"What do you—" Tatters went rigid as Sir Reginald took a step closer to them.

"Winnie," the great steed said. "Who are you talking to?"

"My friend Tatters."

"What *friend*?" Black Knight breathed hotly.

Tatters's eyes flashed with confusion. "The horses are your *friends*?"

Winnie faltered. "Just like you are."

When Tatters squeaked and disappeared into the depths of the hold, Winnie called after him. "Come back! They won't hurt you!"

"Stop speaking the enemy's language, Bear!" Black Knight neighed furiously.

"Could Tatters and the horses understand what each other were saying?" Cole asked.

"No. Because if you're not listening, it's impossible to hear. If you believe that somebody is so different from you that

you can't possibly have anything in common, you'll never be able to hear them no matter what they say. That was the way with the rats and horses. And that's how it is in war."

Cole thought. "Is that why Winnie could talk to anybody?"

"That's right. She had an open heart. Harry had a heart like that too."

"If that's true," Cole said, tracing his Bear's mouth with a finger, "why can't I talk to animals?"

I considered the question. "Maybe you can."

"Can we get a dog?"

I went back to the story.

"Traitor!" Black Knight shook with rage.

The *tip-tap* of tiny feet approached again, and Winnie called for Tatters once more. But now the pitter-patter multiplied and spread like the sound of a growing downpour.

An army of rats descended around your Bear, their eyes

glowing red in the darkness. Tatters crawled from between them. "You don't deserve to be a rat!" His snout quivered.

Your Bear hung her head. "I'm not a rat," she admitted. "I'm a bear."

"Stay away, you poisonous devils!" seethed the horses, jostling in place.

"Rat murderers!" chattered the rats in their own way.

The tension rose until a line of rats charged beneath the horses' legs. Black Knight reared up violently.

Winnie strained at her chain. "STOP!"

At that moment, the door to the hold swung open, and a shaft of light flooded in. Tatters and the rest of the rats scattered at once.

Dixon came down the ramp and rushed to Winnie's side.

"I heard the Colonel locked you down here," he said, running his big hands through her fur. "Winnie, you're shaking."

Once he'd convinced himself she was okay, he turned

his attention to the mounts. "Black Knight, what's wrong?" Right away, he realized how sick some of them were.

While Dixon tended to the horses, and discovered what the problem was, and went about changing their feed, your Bear stayed curled up with her face buried in the fur of her chest. Not since Mama died had she felt so hopeless and alone.

Late that night, Dixon snuck back to the hold, unhooked Winnie's chain, put a finger to his lips, and whispered, "Shhhh. Don't tell the Colonel." Then he threw a burlap sack over your Bear.

With her balled up at the bottom of the sack, he carried her out of the hold. Her shoulder bumped lightly against his leg as he made his way through the ship.

Dixon stopped. Someone was coming toward them.

"Sir!" Dixon said.

"Are you on patrol, Private?"

"No, sir!"

"What are you doing out of quarters? What do you have in that bag?"

Dixon lifted the sack. "Rats caught in the horses' feed, sir. It's swarming with them down there."

"Dead or alive?"

"Excuse me, sir?"

"I asked you, Private, whether the rats you have in that sack are dead or alive?"

Dixon hesitated. "Alive, sir."

There was a long pause. Winnie stayed still. "I suppose they're sleeping," the officer said. Then, very slowly, he said, "You're not stealing rations, are you, Private?"

Something hard—the butt of a gun—jabbed Winnie through the burlap, and in pain and shock, she thrashed all four paws in a wild flurry that made the outside of the sack look like rats were scrambling inside.

"I wish you hadn't woken them up, sir," said Dixon.

"Get rid of them!" the officer growled. "That's an order!"

Dixon opened the sack as soon as the officer had

gone. "You okay, Winnipeg?" He felt Winnie's sides to make sure nothing was broken before cinching the sack up again and carrying on.

A door swished around them, and the sharp smell of the ship's hospital seeped through the burlap. Winnie's heart beat faster as Harry's scent found her nose.

"Is that Winnie?" whispered Brodie in the bottom bunk.

It's me! Winnie wanted to roar.

"I brought you a visitor, Harry," whispered Dixon, setting the sack down on the thin mattress of the top bunk.

The sack fell open, and Winnie poked her head out, and there was Harry, blearily grinning at her with chalky white lips.

"Oh, Winnie!" Harry said. "Your breath is foul!"

In the night, Winnie lay her head on Harry's chest, and when he turned on his side, she rested her chin on his arm, and when he pulled his arm away, she draped herself over his legs, and when he kicked her off and turned onto his stomach, she climbed onto his back, and when he turned over suddenly and began wrestling the sheets from her, a swift kick from below jogged their bunk. "What are you doing up there, dancing?" Brodie whispered loudly. "I'm trying to sleep down here!"

Harry sighed and sat up. "Winnie," he said very softly. "We have to find a way to share the bed. I'm too hot, I don't feel well, and I need some room."

Winnie rubbed her head against his hand. "I just want to be cozy."

"I know you like to be close," whispered Harry.

She and Harry moved around, trying to find the best arrangement. In the end, he lay on his side, with Winnie curled up in the hollow at the back of his knees—close enough to be cozy but contained enough not to crowd him.

And as both of them were drifting off, comfortable at last, something like an idea flittered across the night sky of your Bear's mind.

Winnie snuck from Harry's cot before dawn the next morning, crawling beneath the lower bunks and pressing the swinging door with her paws to open it. When she heard voices around one corner, she skittered up the wall, letting three soldiers pass just underneath her, before she continued on her way. She stopped in the Valley of Fallen Peas to pick up a few fat green ones, climbed down two ladders, crept past the corridor where, even at that hour, men were feeding the furnaces, and found the storeroom where Tatters made his nest.

"Go away!" Tatters squeaked, turning his back to her and tearing some shreds of cloth with his teeth.

Winnie rolled the peas in his direction. "Hungry?"

Tatters grabbed them quickly before hunching down to eat. Over his shoulder, he said, "Are you really a bear? I thought bears were imaginary."

"I am," admitted Winnie. "Will you come with me?"

"I'm not going anywhere with you!" Tatters snapped. But then he scuttled a few steps backward to be closer to her. "Where are you off to?"

"I'm going to see the horses."

"Hah!" wheezed Tatters. "Why would I do that? Horses and rats have been enemies for as long as anyone can remember!"

"Maybe they don't need to be."

"No rat could trust a horse!"

"Just like no rat could be friends with a bear?"

Tatters scratched his whiskers. "Fine. But only because you brought me peas." And he followed Winnie up through a crack near the ceiling.

"What is your proposal?" asked Sir Reginald in the hold once Winnie had convinced the mounts to listen in spite of Black Knight's objections. The horses shuffled impatiently.

Tatters crept forward, trembling, and raised his whiskers. "Horses have to stop killing rats. A horse stepped on my cousin Bobo and she died."

Sir Reginald took this in. "It is unfortunate about your cousin, but we horses must protect ourselves."

"From what!?" squeaked Tatters. He ran back and forth in front of the mounts. "Rats are tiny compared to you!"

Black Knight stamped his hooves. "Can't you see how ill you've made us!"

"We are sick from your filth," Victoria whinnied weakly.

"What do you mean?" Tatters curled one of his whiskers. "All we do is forage for food."

"It is your droppings in our feed that make us sick," explained Sir Reginald.

The little rat's ears twitched and he scratched the back of his head. "I didn't know that." He wriggled his nose. "The only reason horses go wild around us is because they're worried about getting sick?"

The horses bobbed their heads.

Victoria hiccupped in a baffled way. "So rats are just looking for food?"

Her sister, Alberta, blinked in wonder. "They're not trying to kill us, after all."

Tatters and the mounts communed for a long time. They had never understood one another before, horses and rats. They talked about food, that thing that all animals worry over. Tatters was sorry they were sick.

"Is our feed the only food you can eat?" asked Sir Reginald.

Tatters shook her head. "We rats will eat anything. We're not picky. The ship has lots to eat."

Inspired by what Harry had done in the night, Winnie gave a little cough and opened her mouth. "Maybe there's a way for you both to get what you need."

The horses and Tatters looked at Winnie, then at one another.

Tatters sniffed the air thoughtfully. "Maybe I could stop eating in the hold?" Then he raised his eyes and stood up tall, as if he had made a decision. "I promise not to forage in the hold."

A skeptical snort erupted from Black Knight. "One rat won't make a difference."

"It's true." Tatters turned to Winnie. "There's hundreds more besides me."

"Then you'll have to remind them to eat somewhere else when you see them," Winnie told both the horses and Tatters. "Now that you know."

"We will not harm you," Sir Reginald told Tatters. Black Knight nodded.

Sir Reginald flicked his white tail twice, and Tatters gave four tugs on one whisker, and that was how the Truce between Horses and Rats on the SS *Manitou* came to pass.

Cole shifted beside me in bed so he and his Bear were both looking up at me. "Do you think there will ever be a time when there's no more war?"

I sighed. "I don't know. As long as animals have roamed the earth, they've fought—over food, over land, over everything. But maybe if we were better at under-standing each other, there would be less fighting."

Cole pressed the top of his Bear's head down in a nod-ding way. "That's what we think too."

That was the day Harry finally started to feel better. When he got out of the hospital, he found your Bear sniffing around the door to the ship's butcher and brought her to stay in his cabin once more.

A few nights later, he took Winnie to play on the deck, as she liked to do.

She ran from him and sat right on the prow of the ship, letting her ears flap in the wind.

Something scurried up beside her, and Winnie lifted a paw to let Tatters creep in front of her so her body shielded him from the full force of the wind, and to-gether they sat looking out.

Winnie invited him to join her on the next part of her journey, but Tatters just twitched his whiskers. "This ship is my home. Besides, I have to be ready for the next batch of horses. It's up to me to keep the peace."

"You are a very brave rat," Winnie told him.

"So are you."

"Except I'm a bear."

"Whatever you say." Tatters shrugged. "You'll always be my Rat."

Winnie licked Tatters's sea-salty head.

"Do you see that?" squeaked Tatters.

That's when Winnie noticed a blacker strip of sky on the horizon, dotted by clusters of lights. She had thought they were just more stars in the sky.

"It's land," Tatters told her.

The coast of England was finally in sight.

From the Woods, to the cabin, to White River, to the train, to Valcartier, to the ship, to this moment: Your Bear had made it all the way across the ocean.

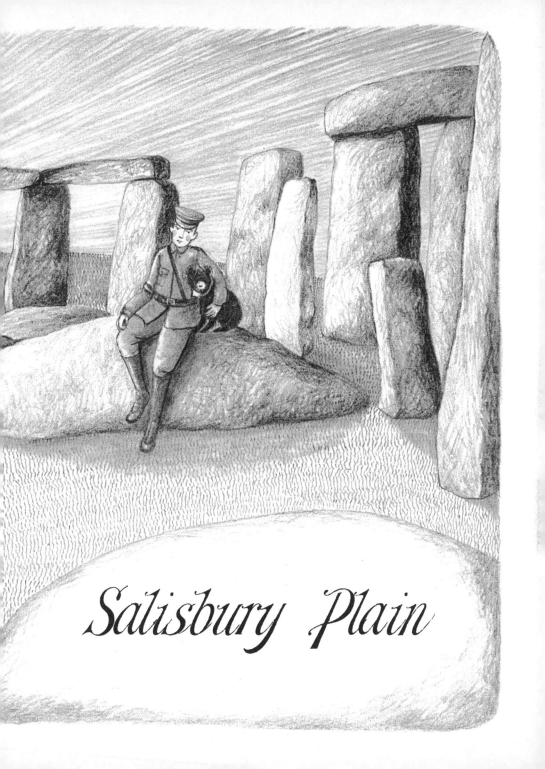

Salisbury Plain

October 15, 1914

Arrived in England.

$\mathcal{W}$hen they got off the ship,
Winnie found that the whole port of Plymouth had
turned up to celebrate her going As Far As Any Bear
Had Ever Gone! The gates of the dockyard were
thronged with people cheering her arrival.

A white banner with hand-painted red letters hung
from the gates: WELCOME CANADIAN TROOPS!

Harry, Brodie, Dixon, Edgett, and Winnie marched together in the long parade of soldiers and horses that wound its way through the cobblestone streets from the seaside to the train station in the center of town.

"We'll take the train to Salisbury Plain," Harry told the boys over the shouts of the crowd. "And continue our preparations there."

"How long until we go where the action is?" yelled Dixon.

"It shouldn't be long now," Harry shouted.

The way was lined with people, voices raised, arms outstretched, waving newspapers and holding out gifts to the soldiers. A bald man with an apron forced a pair of oranges into Dixon's hands. A stooped old woman with a kerchief on her head reached up, pulled down Harry's face by the cheeks, and kissed him wetly on each one. "Bless you for coming to our aid!" she cried.

Brodie paused to strike up a conversation with a smiling young woman in a pale blue coat. He made a trade with her: his pin, pewter and shaped like a maple leaf, for her button, brass and etched with an image of the

King. She held Brodie's pin to her lips as Edgett pulled him away.

"I told you the Canadians were fierce," someone said, elbowing his neighbor. "Look what they brought with them! A bear!"

A little boy with a teddy bear ran into the street. He pumped it out at Winnie. "That's a real bear, isn't it?!"

Harry stooped down. "It is! A real North American black bear."

The boy backed away. "Is it friendly?"

When Winnie brushed her nose against the boy's hand, he shrieked with delight and hopped up and down before carefully patting her head.

Once the citizens of Plymouth saw that Winnie could be approached, they held out all kinds of things to her: grapes and hard candies, which she ate with the wrappers still on, and even a few cigarettes, which Harry snatched from her mouth not a moment too soon.

Winnie noticed a monkey with a long tail and a tiny top hat sitting on the shoulder of a man who had one eye opened much wider than the other, which was nearly squinted shut. The monkey gave a cheeky tip of his hat to your Bear as the man struck up singing in a strong, quavering voice. Within moments, the troops and the crowd all joined in.

> *It's a long way to Tipperary,*
> *It's a long way to go.*
> *It's a long way to Tipperary*
> *To the sweetest girl I know!*

Everyone knew the song. It made Winnie bounce as she walked.

October 18, 1914
Arrived at Salisbury 10 AM.

Your Bear loved the water, so rain was her favorite sort of weather. But among all the different kinds of rain—from the waterfall-like torrents that made ferns shine greener in the Woods to the early-morning mistings of Valcartier—the kind of hard-driving rain that drenched Salisbury Plain was her favorite kind of all.

For weeks on end, bulging drops of water pelted from the gray sky, striking up muddy blasts that turned the ground to mush. It rained and it rained and it rained. While the men trudged along with their heads down, Winnie raced and romped, slid and sloshed, so that brown mud covered her black fur like a second coat.

"At least Winnie likes this weather," said Brodie as they waded after her across camp one morning.

"She might be the only one in the whole army," said Dixon. "My toes feel like they're swimming in ice."

"I like to imagine I'm walking on piles of wet

sandwiches," said Brodie, pulling his coat tightly around him to protect against the bitter wind.

Edgett said, "Soldiers at the Front have been having problems with their feet in the damp and the cold. Trench foot, they call it."

"I'm already out of dry socks," noted Dixon.

"Trench foot?" said Harry. "We'd better check the horses."

He led Winnie and the others to the edge of camp, where the mounts stood shivering halfway up to their bony knees in mud. They had been forced to move every few days, farther and farther from the center of camp, because there was no shelter for them, and whenever they took a step, their hooves churned in the mire and sunk deeper down, creating a soupy sea.

"Sir Reginald," Harry said.

"Captain." Sir Reginald gave a solemn bob of his head, the rain streaming down his muzzle. "Mascot Winnie."

Harry patted him firmly all along his body with a gloved hand before moving along to Black Knight.

"I like the rain," Winnie had to admit. "Do you like the rain?"

"Oh," Black Knight said with a grim flick of his eyes. "If only we could all be bears."

Harry bent and plucked one of Black Knight's hooves from the muck. He wiped the back of it with his gloved hand, trying to gain a clear look.

Winnie glimpsed an oozing red sore on the back of Black Knight's ankle.

Harry winced. "We've left them standing around in the wet too long."

"Does it hurt?" Winnie wondered.

"It does." Black Knight nodded. "But we are headed to war. This is nothing compared to what's to come."

Winnie watched warily as a pair of officers plodded past, their rifles slung over their shoulders.

Harry and the boys spent the whole day wrapping

the horses' legs in bandages to keep them dry. The mounts who were shivering got blankets, which were immediately soaked but better than nothing.

Outside their tent, Winnie gave herself a blissful shake that splattered Harry's uniform. He yelled at her before grabbing a filthy towel and roughly rubbing the rest of the mud from her body.

Inside, he threw the towel on the floor and didn't take off his big boots because everything was already slick and grimy. When he noticed water streaming from a seam in the wall he had already mended, he sat on the edge of the bed and hung his head.

Carefully, Harry unfolded the piece of oilskin he wrapped his diary in to keep it dry. He licked the end of his pencil and was about to touch it to the page when a howl of wind shook the canvas wall and the lantern flame flickered out.

Harry cursed! He flung the pencil to the floor, then spent a long time feeling around with his boot in the dark looking for it, twice kicking Winnie out of the way.

Finally, he gave up and turned in, facing the wall, without scratching your Bear once. Winnie could hear Harry shivering under his thin, damp blanket. When he started making sounds, she poked her head up to check on him. Winnie touched his shoulder with her nose, and Harry turned and pulled her into him, gasping between sobs.

Words ran out of his mouth. "I was so sick on the ship, and I don't know what I'm doing in charge of all these men, and it's one thing after another with the horses, and instead of taking care of them, I've already let so many die." He hiccupped. "I've never felt so cold and wet in my life, and I came here from Winnipeg, one of the coldest places on earth."

His voice dropped to a frightened whisper. "If I can't get by now, what will happen at the Front?"

Winnie knew what it was like to be scared. Calmly, she licked the tears from his face and laid her head on his side.

The storm of Harry's breathing slowly cleared. He wiped his nose on your Bear. "Chin up, Colebourn," he said to himself in a strong voice. "Do your duty."

Winnie put her paw on top of his hand, and he pulled his hand away and laid it on top of hers, then she thumped hers down again, trying to catch his before he pulled it away, and they played like that until finally Harry laughed.

"Oh, silly bear!" he said, scratching her neck in that special place. "How I do love you!"

Winnie took her duty very seriously.

Wherever she went in Salisbury, she brightened men's spirits, no matter how soggy their spirits were. She added *Stand guard!* and *Roll over!* to *Attention!*,

Salute!, *Forward!*, and *Double march!* She was always careful to obey a commander's orders before sniffing his hands or pockets looking for a little something.

She became known as a fierce competitor at tug-of-war, and her skills at hide-and-seek gave rise to a small gambling ring. Brodie made out handsomely.

She was honored when a British officer taught her to peel and eat an orange after she'd retrieved his riding crop from the mud.

But her finest hour may have been when Edgett and Dixon drove a log into the ground outside Harry's tent. "There you go, Winnipeg," said Dixon. "Now you have your very own Post in the army."

She rubbed her scent on it and made scratch marks so there could be no mistaking whose it was. Several times a day, Winnie climbed her Post to stand watch over camp.

Your Bear was Mascot of the Second Canadian Infantry Brigade, and she proudly attended her Post.

One evening, Harry and Dixon tied Winnie up outside the YMCA tent while they went inside, and she found herself tethered beside a four-legged creature who had a scrawny white beard and a pair of curved horns that rose like a split trunk from his head. His back was draped in a coat of scarlet flannel with an army patch sewn on it.

"I'm Winnie," said Winnie with her nose in the air. "Second Infantry Brigade. Bear."

The animal showed its teeth. "Bill, Fifth Infantry Battalion. Goat."

"I didn't know there were any other animals here besides horses," said Winnie.

"Aye, we are a rare bunch," the goat said proudly. "Have you not met the carrier pigeons? They're fearless, they are. They've already started flying missions across the Channel."

Winnie had been wondering about those fast gray fliers she'd seen over camp.

"How did you get in the army?" she asked.

"The troop train came through Saskatchewan, and the Curwain family saw fit to enlist me."

"I started on the train too!" Winnie cocked her head. "Did you come over on one of the big ships?"

"I did." Bill nodded. He leaned closer. "Did you get sick?"

"I didn't."

"Me neither."

They looked at each other with respect as the rain began to fall once more.

A question tiptoed inside Winnie. "Are you scared? Of the War?"

The goat paused. "I wouldn't be alive if I wasn't." His nostrils blew a plume of steam into the drizzle. "But there is no bravery on this earth without fear. I shall stand with my men till the end, as they would do for me."

Harry and Dixon came back and untied Winnie. Before they led her away, she raised her chin to Bill, who butted the air with his horns. "Good luck," they told each other.

Your Bear never saw Bill again.

"You made that up!" complained Cole. "There wasn't a goat like that."

"Oh yes, there was. There was a billy goat from Broadview, Saskatchewan, who came to England on the same convoy as Winnie and trained on Salisbury Plain and fought with the Fighting Fifth in France. He once got court-martialed for eating the master list of soldiers, but they forgave him when they found him standing guard over a Prussian fighter in a bomb crater. He was promoted to the rank of sergeant. Later in the War, he butted three soldiers into a trench a split second before a shell exploded on the spot where they'd been standing. He could

hear it coming; he saved their lives. Sergeant Bill re-
ceived the Victory Medal before returning home to
Canada."

"No way," said Cole.

"Winnie's isn't the only incredible story, you know."

Winnie sat before Harry and Brodie in one of the long ditches where the soldiers of Salisbury Plain practiced living in trenches. Looking down at them from the edge of the pit was Colonel Currie, who was standing beside a large man with hooded eyes shaded by a peaked cap with a medal on it. His upper lip was hidden by a mustache that looked like a giant caterpillar.

"We're going to play a little game of hide-and-seek for the General, Winnie," said Harry nervously. He shook the wet from his hands, squatted in the mud, and gave her neck a good rub.

He plucked a soiled gray sock from his pocket and handed it to Brodie, who dangled it before Winnie's nose. "Mmmmm," Brodie said in an exaggerated way.

Winnie wagged her tongue.

"I'm going to hide this," said Brodie, twirling the sock through the air. "And you're going to find it."

Winnie flattened her ears to say she understood.

Harry held Winnie's leash as Brodie backed away slowly, swinging the sock in one hand. At the end of the trench, he turned and ducked into an opening in the wall that looked like the mouth of a cave and was gone.

"Wait now," Harry told Winnie quietly. "We need to give him time to get away."

The General coughed with impatience. "I assure you, Colonel Currie," said the British commander, "there is only one bloodhound in the animal kingdom."

The Colonel took the words in with a brief nod. "I agree, General Alderson. But there is also only one Winnie the Bear."

Harry clapped his hands together. "Go find it, Winnie! GO!"

Off she ran into the underground tunnel. On the uneven walls, some men had already carved their names.

When the tunnel forked, she went one way, where she found an empty condensed milk tin and licked it clean. But then she realized she'd lost the scent of the sock, so she went back and tried the other way. She came to a widening in the tunnel, where a group of four soldiers were playing cards by the light of a lantern. They scooted back against the walls in alarm as she sniffed at their feet.

Having assured herself that none of them had the sock, she moved on. But on second thought, she returned. "Is one of you chewing toffee? I like toffee." Before they could respond, she remembered: *The sock!*

She raced along on her hunt. A dim light appeared up ahead, and she came out into a trench much like the one where she'd started.

Winnie stopped. She breathed in and out deeply. She

scrambled up the ladder leading out of the trench and looked around, lifting her nose carefully to pick through the scents of the night one by one. There it was!

And off she went, winding between tents and under the water trough where the men washed.

But then, without warning, the scent was gone. She retraced her steps, her nose just above the ground, and went back and turned around. She smelled Harry and the Colonel and Brodie and the General. There they were, peeking out from behind a nearby tent.

She had an idea and returned to where the smell stopped, near the camp flagpole.

She dug but found nothing. She sat down to have a think.

"Do you concede defeat?" announced the General.

It must be here somewhere, thought Winnie. That's when the memory of the Colonel, searching their tent in Valcartier, sprouted into her head.

And so your Bear looked straight up.

At the top of the flagpole was the flag of Great Britain. But beneath it hung something small and droopy, barely visible against the night sky.

Winnie scaled the flagpole like a shot and snatched the sock in her mouth.

It's Higher Than Any Sock Has Ever Gone! thought your Bear.

Down below, Harry and Brodie were jumping up and down in a happy way.

"I win," said the Colonel to the General. "It appears you owe my men fresh socks."

The General's caterpillar of a mustache was very excited. "Colonel, do you know what we could do with a nose like that? We could sniff out explosives! We could hunt German spies—"

"Sir!" Harry said as Winnie took her place at his side. The General scowled at the interruption. "I'm sorry, sir. She's not that sort of bear."

Instead of speaking to Harry, the General turned to his commanding officer. "Is that so, Colonel Currie?"

The Colonel looked briefly at Harry, then at Winnie, then back at the General.

"Presently," he sputtered, "as you can see—"

The General cut him off. "Where we are going, the bear will not have a choice."

Darkness on Salisbury Plain came earlier and earlier, and the wind grew colder still.

"What do you mean, all movement has stopped?" said Brodie, warming his hands over a stove outside while Winnie rolled around in the mud nearby.

Edgett's impassive face was all angles and shadows in the stove's firelight. "Both armies have been racing north all fall, trying to outflank each other. The Front is four hundred miles long now, and there's no place else to go without falling into the sea."

"It's like we put a giant crack down the middle of Europe," said Dixon. "We can throw ourselves down it or stare at each other over it, but no one can cross it now. Seventy-five thousand men fell at Ypres this month and we didn't gain an inch."

"Neither did they," said Edgett. "That's what's important."

"They should let us have a go at it," said Brodie, lifting his cap and smoothing his dark hair. "The horses are ready. We're no good to anyone sitting here."

The men looked over at Harry, who hadn't said a word. He was gazing down at Winnie in a far-off way.

Dixon said, "What do you say, Captain? Isn't it time we had our orders?"

Harry lifted his pale eyes. "Soon enough."

On a rare rainless morning, the boys lined up to have their pictures taken with your Bear.

Dixon stood beside Winnie and forced a smile, but the man with the camera wasn't ready. Dixon exhaled.

"When I moved to Canada to find work, I left my love behind in Maidenhead, not two hours from here," he told Winnie while they waited. "I don't know why I haven't written Louise since we landed. I hate to worry her, is all. But now I'll send her this picture, Winnipeg, and when she sees it, she'll have a good laugh and know not to worry." He grimaced and shifted in his boots. Then he shouted, "Take the blasted picture!" Winnie startled and the camera clicked.

Edgett sat stiffly on the ground and took her in his lap. "You're not afraid, are you?" he whispered into her neck, so quietly that only Winnie could hear. "You're going to be just fine; you're going to live through this War and make it home to sleep in a warm bed and eat roast beef for breakfast. Isn't that right?" The cameraman called, "Hold still!" *Click.* Before he got to his feet, Edgett briskly rubbed one forearm up and down on Winnie's back three times. "I'm not superstitious," he said.

Brodie knelt before her with an apple and two stones. He pretended to hold the fruit out to her but snatched it back, took a bite, and started juggling. She batted frantically at the air with her paws until the two stones fell in the mud. But the apple was still held aloft in Brodie's hand. He handed it over.

"Very funny." Winnie took a bite. They were both smiling in that photo.

Colonel Currie, Major Onions, and some officers Winnie had never smelled before came and sat on wooden chairs. The Colonel held her leash in his gloved hands while Major Onions tried to get Winnie's attention with a stale biscuit. She averted her nose.

Harry stood in the back.

"Are you sure you won't change your mind, Captain Colebourn?" said Colonel Currie as the photographer held up his hand. "It seems a shame to carry on without our mascot."

"I'm sure, sir," Harry said.

Winnie jerked her head away from Major Onions so the photographer caught only her side, while Harry looked on without a smile.

Your Bear knew something wasn't right. The boys were unusually quiet as they gathered outside Harry's tent before dawn.

No one would even look at her.

Harry pulled up in the driver's seat of the Colonel's motorcar. He covered the backseat in a horse blanket and held the door open for her, but she wouldn't get in.

"I'm not getting in," Winnie said by lying down in the mud.

When Dixon tried to pick her up in his hands, she struggled. It took both he and Brodie to force her inside and Edgett to slam the door.

"No!" Her claws scratched wildly at the window as Harry started the engine. Winnie butted the glass with her head as she watched the boys recede down the road, their heads bowed, their hands in their pockets.

Now the car was passing the muddy field where the horses were, and Winnie's nose pressed against the streaked glass. "Sir Reginald! Black Knight! Alberta! Victoria!" She willed the mounts to look at her.

Only Sir Reginald's great dark eyes found hers, and he nodded a proud salute. Then he shook his tail sadly and dropped his gaze as Harry sped up and drove out of camp.

Winnie was very upset. She crashed from the back-seat to the front as the car made its way across the flat plain. Finally, she snapped at Harry's ear and clawed at his face, and he nearly ran off the road. "Winnie!" Harry cried. "Stop it!"

The motorcar pulled over with a jerk and a screech, and Harry yanked her after him by the leash out of the car.

They were in front of a great broken circle of giant stones.

"Do you know what Stonehenge is?" I asked Cole.

"Yes," said Cole, smoothing the blanket around his stuffed animal. "But I'm not sure Bear does."

"It's an ancient, mysterious place. It was built thousands of years ago on Salisbury Plain and no one knows how or why. How did they get such big stones there? Why are they set up the way they are? Some people think it was for looking at the sun and the stars. Maybe it had healing powers. That's where Harry and Winnie were."

"It's not safe for you where we're going, Winnie," Harry said as the ancient stones loomed in the gloom. "It's not safe for anyone."

Winnie growled in an angry way, but Harry shook his head. "I didn't rescue you in White River to endanger you now," he told her. "I'm taking you someplace safe."

The top of the sun's head was peeking up yellow and red through the gathering of stones. And all at once, the energy left your Bear.

She rubbed her side against Harry's boot. "I'm scared of losing you."

Harry's hand came down to stroke her neck. "You have to be brave," he told her. "We all have to be brave."

As the sun's first rays spilt onto the plain, memories lit up inside Winnie. She had climbed the white-trunked tree, and spoken to squirrels, and carried on after Mama died, and trusted the boy, and left the Woods, and gone on the train, and befriended the horses, and faced the Colonel, and helped stop the stampede, and crossed the ocean, and made peace between horses and rats.

But the Great War demanded more bravery still.

They walked to the middle of the stone circle, and sat together in the center of Stonehenge, where Harry scratched the special place on her neck, and they watched the sun come up, both of them gathering the courage to do what must be done.

London

*A*s they drove into the City, the tall buildings looked down on them.

People in buses, children waving madly, the heavy eyes of a policeman peering in. They passed Buckingham Palace and drove beneath Marble Arch, but Winnie didn't care where her journey was taking her now. She rested her head beside Harry's leg on the front seat, her nose just touching his knee.

Harry stopped the car, and they walked through Regent's Park down the middle of a broad gravel pathway lined by trees. The jumbled scents of countless strange animals closed in around your Bear.

And there they were: the entrance to the gardens of the Zoological Society of London.

A slender woman in a dark purple dress came out to meet them. Her hat looked like it was made of dark blue straw, and a large blue handbag hung at her side.

"You must be Captain Colebourn. I'm Silvie Saunders, the new zookeeper." She shook Harry's hand.

"You're new?" asked Harry.

"Since Keeper Graves enlisted." She bent down. "And you, young lady, must be Winnipeg," she said, holding out her hand. Winnie looked at it: Her palm was as pink as tinned salmon.

Harry got down on both knees to talk to your Bear. "This is going to be your home for a while, Winnie. It won't be long, just until the fighting's done and I can take you back to Winnipeg." His dimple quivered, and he took her head in his hands and brought his nose close to hers.

"Don't worry," he said in a voice turning husky. "No matter what happens, you'll always be my Bear."

Winnie breathed in his scent before he cleared his throat and suddenly stood and handed her leash to Miss Saunders. "Take care of her."

"You have my word," said Miss Saunders. "Though I don't think she's the one whose safety we need to worry about, Captain Colebourn."

Winnie's heart gasped for breath like a fish on dry land as Harry started to walk away, but Miss Saunders stopped him with her voice. "When are you coming to visit?"

Harry seemed surprised by the question. He glanced up at the cloudy sky, then brought his pale, clear eyes back to your Bear. "On my next leave. Though I don't know when that will be."

Miss Saunders placed her hand gently atop Winnie's head.

"We shall be waiting," she said.

"I think you'll be pleased with your lodgings, Winnie," said Miss Saunders, leading her past the duck pond inside the entrance to the Zoo. "We've got you a place on the Mappin Terraces. They just opened last year, and I think you'll find them quite roomy and natural."

Winnie found herself blinking up at a small jagged mountain that didn't smell anything like real rock. Cut into it were tiers called Terraces. And along the outside of each Terrace was a walkway with people strolling along.

Miss Saunders sang, "Good afternooooooon, beauties!" to the hot-pink flamingos in the pond at the bottom of the Mappin Terraces. "I'd like you to meet your new neighbor. This is Winnie the Bear. Winnie, meet our fabulous flamingos!"

The birds strutted gracefully before her. But instead of saying hello, Winnie lay down on the ground and put her muzzle on her paws.

"Brighten up, love," one blinked. The others wiggled their necks in agreement.

"You're a lucky bear," flapped another, who had just lifted her head from underwater. "Until last year, the bears lived in a pit, with nothing to do but climb a pole and eat scraps off a stick."

Miss Saunders said, "Let's go up and have a look at the dens, shall we?" They climbed a staircase and turned onto the third walkway on the right. Across from them, on the other side of an empty moat, the Terrace was open to the sky and divided by walls.

The middle of the walkway was clogged by a crowd of people. Miss Saunders squeezed through with Winnie to see what they were all looking at. No one paid much attention to your Bear, because they were too riveted by the antics of the polar bear couple across the way.

The bigger one was pacing back and forth near the back of the den. Above him, a visitor with red cheeks and a feathered hat was leaning over the rear wall, waving a frilly umbrella and calling "Yoo-hoo!" to get his attention. Lazily, the polar bear stuck a claw in one ear and rolled his eyes.

Meanwhile, his female companion sat in a puny puddle of water near the moat, scrubbing her armpits.

With a sudden powerful spring, the male bear rose to his full height—Winnie was stunned because, apart from being white all over, he was more than three times as tall as Mama—and snatched the visitor's umbrella, stripped the fabric from its frame with a sweep of his claws, and pranced about on two legs while holding the mangled umbrella overhead. The crowd roared with laughter.

"Sam," called Miss Saunders in a warning sort of way. "Are you behaving yourself?"

The polar bear dropped to all fours and kicked the umbrella's skeleton away. "Who, me?"

"Sam, Barbara," said Miss Saunders, "I'd like you to meet Winnie. She's from Canada! Sam and Barbara are what you might call celebrities here at the Zoo. Sam likes to steal people's umbrellas."

Sam sauntered to the edge of the moat to get a better look at your Bear.

Winnie sniffed the ground shyly, avoiding his eyes.

"Well, aren't *you* a delightfully plain and quiet bear," Sam drawled.

"He means that as a compliment," said Barbara with a stretch of her neck. "The last bear who lived next door was a Himalayan. What an unworldly racket he made! Welcome to the neighborhood, dear."

Now Miss Saunders was taking Winnie to the end of the walkway and around the side, where she stopped at a dark green metal door and put a key into a lock.

Deep inside the Terraces, Miss Saunders led Winnie

down a dark and gloomy passageway lit by an electric bulb fixed high on the wall. Your Bear tried to be brave, but she trailed behind, walking as slowly as she could.

At the top of a short, steep set of wooden stairs was a closed gate. Sunlight filtered through from the other side.

Winnie understood that they were at a den's back door.

Miss Saunders reached into her bag and pulled out an apple. She showed Winnie into her den, placed the apple on the ground, and, with a kick of her dainty shoe, rolled it farther inside. Winnie followed the apple slowly. Then she heard a lonely *clank* as Miss Saunders closed the gate.

"Wait," Cole interrupted, as if realizing something for the first time. "Winnie had to live in a cage at the Zoo?"

"The Mappin Terraces weren't really a cage," I said.

"Was she allowed to go outside?" he asked. "Outside, outside."

"No."

"Could she walk around the Zoo? Could she visit other animals?"

"No."

Cole crossed his Bear in his arms. "That's wrong."

"It's what happened."

"Locking Winnie up in a zoo is NOT RIGHT! She deserved to be free!"

"I agree with you," I said softly as I wrapped my arms around him and his Bear. "But it's the only place Harry thought he could leave her."

"She must have hated it," Cole said bitterly.

Your Bear *hated* the Zoo.

She would trudge around the edges of her den, ignoring the spectators who called to her, and lick half-heartedly at the puddle of water.

She slept nearly all the time.

Days stretched into months. One new moon after another bloomed into fullness, then died away.

Sometimes she would crawl right up to the front of her den and drape her nose over the edge of the empty moat, watching the passersby watching her. Every day, hundreds of people stood there, waiting for Winnie to do something. The only time her ears perked up was when a green uniform appeared in the crowd.

Harry, is that you? she would think.

It never was. It was never Brodie, or Dixon, or Edgett, or Colonel Currie, or any of her boys. It was just one more soldier visiting the Zoo to take his mind off the War. Sometimes he wore a bandage around his head or on his arm or leg. Sometimes he had no legs at all.

She was comforted, at least a little, by Miss Saunders, who took to coming into her den and giving her a baby's bottle of condensed milk like Harry used to do. While your Bear drank in silence, Miss Saunders petted her fur gently and sang in a sweet whisper.

> *Keep the home fires burning,*
> *While your hearts are yearning,*
> *Though your lads are far away*
> *They dream of home.*

> *There's a silver lining*
> *Through the dark clouds shining,*
> *Turn the dark cloud inside out*
> *'Til the boys come home!*

April 19, 1915

Germans shell town and kill 4 soldiers in Grand Place. Saw aeroplane fall. Stay in cellar under large grocery store for several hours. Tremendous shelling.

April 21, 1915

*Shelled out of my billet & lost everything. Stayed at no.
16 vet mobile station. Have supper with English cavalry.
Many killed.*

Warm.

April 22, 1915

Shell bursts almost at my feet.

*Germans gas French soldiers who retreat en masse. Hundreds of civilians and soldiers streaming down road out of
Ypres. Old men carrying their wives on their backs.*

Terrible scenes.

Canadian soldiers hold on grimly against great odds.

April 23, 1915

Lost everything. Returned to Ypres under heavy shell fire to try to save some of my things. Attempt failed.

April 24, 1915

Germans attack. Terrible fighting. Canadian troops hanging on.
Recovered coat from ruins.
7000 Canadian casualties.

April 26, 1915

Severe fighting all day. Visit lines in morning. Bombs drop on Poperinge. Close call in afternoon with Dixon.

"Winnie," said Miss Saunders after plying her with a custard tart one day. "I'm worried about you. You've been down."

Winnie blinked at her from where she lay.

"I was thinking. How would you like some visitors?"

Winnie sighed and turned away.

"I know it's not *customary*, but you're not a customary bear. Even with Sam and Barbara, we'd be worried about someone getting hurt. But I don't believe you could hurt a fruit fly, could you?"

Winnie thought. She got to her feet and went and

sniffed at Miss Saunders's handbag. "Do you have anything more to eat?"

Miss Saunders smiled. "That's the spirit," she said, opening her bag. "What sort of guest doesn't bring a little something extra?"

The next day, there was someone standing beside Miss Saunders at the gate: an elderly woman wearing a long coat who was not much taller than Winnie. Wisps of white hair peeked out from beneath the brim of her ornate hat. Around her neck and in the lobes of her ears were stones that sparkled brightly even in the gloom of the tunnel.

"Winnie," said Miss Saunders. "I'd like you to meet Mrs. Mappin. She's one of our patron saints."

"Nonsense," the woman said. "It was my husband, John, and the silversmiths of Mappin & Webb who made all this possible. I'm just a lover of animals."

Miss Saunders opened the gate and pressed a bottle of milk into Mrs. Mappin's frail hand. Mrs. Mappin moved toward your Bear slowly, with a doubtful look back to Miss Saunders. Winnie stood and went to meet her.

"Is that for me?" wondered Winnie, her lips searching for the bottle.

Mrs. Mappin drew in her breath when Winnie began to feed. "My, you are a beauty," she said, tipping the bottle. She stroked Winnie's neck with her other trembling hand.

Mrs. Mappin came to see your Bear throughout that spring, sometimes twice a day. She fed Winnie, and held her, and petted her. Most of all, she talked to her.

"Why, I was just a *girl*," Mrs. Mappin said. "But when John said, 'You know, Ellen, a silver goblet is worthless without something to fill it,' there wasn't a thing I could do but fall for him." Winnie remembered Harry's hand reaching out to her under the bench at the station in White River.

"You can't imagine the uproar when John and my brother George set up shop down the road from John's brothers," Mrs. Mappin said on another visit. "They were furious! But John felt he had to prove himself." Winnie thought of Harry, face-to-face with the Colonel the morning he became Orderly Officer of the Day.

"The maharaja wanted a bedroom done completely in silver. When it was finished, John put the whole room up in the store window, and they had to shut down the street for the crowds! The police made him take it down because they were sure someone would steal it." Winnie remembered the glittering smells of the mess tent at Valcartier, Harry whisking her away in his arms.

"This was his dream, and he held on to see it through. You probably don't know this, because you're a bear, but John left us nearly on the day construction of the Terraces was finished." Winnie recalled Harry's pale, clear eyes as he held her face in his hands before leaving her at the Zoo.

The bottle was empty once more.

Mrs. Mappin blinked as if she were just waking up. "I can't believe it's been almost a year since he passed." Her eyes became shiny, and she blew out a trembling breath. "I miss him very, very much," she said, and it was as if she were speaking for your Bear. But then Mrs. Mappin laughed through her tears: "But you make me feel better, you silly bear."

Winnie sat back. Mrs. Mappin had jogged something loose way up inside her.

As if a nut had fallen from a tree and plunked her on the head, your Bear suddenly remembered her duty.

"That's why I'm here!" Winnie leaned in and stuck her nose right in Mrs. Mappin's face. "I make people feel better!"

When Winnie was jolted awake in her den that night, her first thought was of the horses.

The Terraces were cast in a strange light. It was a cloudless night, the moon nearly full in a way bears can sense, but something wasn't right.

When Winnie looked at the sky, a shiver rippled through her. Something was partly blocking the moon. Droplets were falling from whatever it was, black rain against the dark gray night.

Balls of fire bounced off the horizon suddenly. And then the explosions reached Winnie's ears, and all at once, the sounds of the Zoo rushed in: the alarmed trumpeting of elephants, monkeys screaming, birds calling out to one another.

On the other side of her den's wall, Winnie heard Barbara weeping as Sam tried to comfort her.

Winnie shrank back against her slope. A man on a bicycle rode past the bottom of the Terraces blowing a whistle in short forceful bursts. "Take cover!" he cried between shrieks of his whistle. "Take cover!"

More explosions rattled the City.

Someone ran by on the walkway above your Bear. "It's a zeppelin attack! Get the animals inside!"

"What's a zeppelin?" asked Cole, hiding his Bear under the covers.

"It's a really big blimp."

"It dropped bombs?"

"Yes."

"Did anyone get hurt?"

"Seven people died in that first raid on London, but the Zoo was okay."

Cole pressed his lower lip against the satin edge of his blanket. "I didn't know there were war blimps."

The air still smelled burnt when the first visitors arrived at the Zoo the next morning. Faces were pale. Legs moved stiffly. The whole city was shaken by the attack in the night.

But Winnie was up and ready.

Attention! Salute! Forward! Double march! She marched along on two legs, waving with her nose at the passersby.

On the walkway, a little girl giggled and tugged her distracted mother's hand. The woman looked, and a smile spread across her face.

More and more visitors stopped to point and wave at your Bear. A round-faced boy sitting on his daddy's shoulders clapped for her, kicking his father's chest with his heels. A woman wrapped in colorful scarves waved her hands over her head, and Winnie did the same. A member of the fire brigade threw her a warm bun, and she caught it in midair.

"Winnie," Sam called over the wall, "are you trying to steal my thunder?"

"Thunder?" Winnie dropped onto all fours. "Is that why you need all those umbrellas?"

As spring turned to summer, more special guests were allowed into Winnie's den. Miss Saunders would lead them right up to her gate, introduce them, and let them inside. Winnie would rub her flank against each visitor's leg to greet them.

There was the lanky, cheerful old man with a pale blue work coat and a face that reminded Winnie of Sir Reginald the horse, especially when he laughed. Pfeiffer was his name. Miss Saunders said he visited the Zoo every day except Christmas.

"Winnie!" he'd say. "The hippopotamuses were asking

about you." Their favorite game was Flying Chestnuts. This involved Pfeiffer standing on the other side of the den from your Bear while holding a small greasy paper bag. He'd pitch chestnuts from the bag to her one by one. Those watching from the walkway would count each successful catch in Winnie's mouth. "One! Two! Three! Four!" Winnie once caught seventeen chestnuts in a row, which she thought was probably More Chestnuts Than Any Bear Had Ever Caught.

A large woman with a small chin fed her sardines on strips of toast. Afterward, she sang to Winnie in a high, warbling voice. She was an opera singer, but the Royal Opera House had been shuttered for the War and turned into a furniture warehouse. Winnie danced on two feet as she sang, and the visitors to the Terraces clapped for them both.

Miss Saunders concocted a special drink, especially for when Winnie had guests: Winnie's cocktail, which was one part condensed milk, one part golden syrup, stirred. Whenever she drank one, your Bear rocked on her back and hummed a grand symphony.

One cool, cloudy summer day, Miss Saunders called to Winnie from the gate. Your Bear trotted up, but she didn't recognize who was waiting there at first because his scent was caked with smoke and his hat was missing.

But then she knew all at once and as the gate opened, she jumped up on Harry and very nearly knocked him to the ground.

July 8, 1915

In London all day. Visit Zoo in morning & see Winnie. Afternoon looking round city. Visit bookstore and was measured for jack boots. Also bought watch. Lunch at Lyon's popular restaurant in Piccadilly.

"Oh, Winnie!" Harry cried as she licked his face all over. He tucked in his dimpled chin. "You've gotten so big," he gasped.

Her hind feet stumbled over his boots as she pawed at his chest. "It's you!" She snorted, unable to believe her senses. "It's you!"

"Settle down now," Harry said, and his fingers found that spot behind her neck, and she settled. Harry sank to the ground beside her. She put one paw on top of the hand that wasn't scratching her. He slipped his hand out and put it on top of her paw. She moved her paw on top of his hand. He put his hand on top of her paw. She thumped him hard with both paws.

"Hey," said Harry, pushing aside her nose roughly. "Want to wrestle?"

And so they wrestled. They wrestled the way Mama and your Bear wrestled so long ago and far away, pushing themselves under each other, feeling each other's weight against their shoulders, climbing over each other. Winnie got to standing on Harry's back, but then Harry roared and flung her off into the puddle and jumped on *her* back, and she dragged him around and over the slopes toward the gate as he kicked his feet comically while the crowd cheered them on.

He let go and they both collapsed, panting and smiling dumbly.

The voice of a child on the walkway above asked, "Did Winnie win?"

As Harry lay there, blinking and breathing and doing nothing at all, Winnie examined him bottom to top. The sole of one of his boots had come loose; it flapped when she nudged it, though it was tied to the shoe leather above by a tattered strip of bandage. A spiderweb crack marred the watch on Harry's wrist, and there was mist trapped behind its glass. When Winnie listened, its familiar tocking was gone; all she heard was Harry's stomach grumbling. One of his thumbnails was black. She rooted around the top of his head and found a long, thin pink path through his fur.

"We had a close call, Dixon and I," said Harry in an absentminded way. "A sniper's bullet struck my helmet. It sounded like a church bell, but it was just a scratch. A miracle, really." Winnie licked the scar. Very quietly, Harry said, "I don't know why I was the lucky one."

He rubbed his eyes and let out his breath. "It's a horrible business, this War," he said. "But the future of the world depends on us, so we must soldier on. Not for ourselves. For one another. For our children's children's children's children." He stroked your Bear's ear. "Isn't that so?"

Winnie could tell Harry was preparing to leave. Bravely, she nodded.

Harry got to his feet, dusted himself off, and saluted.

Winnie saluted back.

"Miss Saunders!" Harry called. He gave a brisk nod to your Bear. "Take care of London while I'm gone, Winnie."

And then Harry went back to the Front.

The seasons repeated themselves over and over as the War wore on.

At least once a year, Harry would travel from the front lines in France or Belgium to visit your Bear. Winnie grew into a husky grown-up, while Harry got more wiry and compact. When he visited, Winnie noticed a grim determination beneath his smile, though his hands remained as warm as ever. He and the horses saw some of the worst battles of the War. They were part of the charge when the Canadians took Vimy Ridge in 1917. It was a great and terrible victory: more than ten thousand Canadian soldiers killed or wounded in just three days and thousands of horses lost.

There were more zeppelin attacks on London. When the City succeeded in fighting them off, the Germans replaced their blimps with biplane bombers that flew above the clouds like dragonflies. Big guns were set up around London to shoot them down. Winnie grew used to taking cover.

While many places were closed during the War, the Zoo drew larger crowds than ever. Faced with so much hardship and pain, people flocked to see the animals. Millions walked past Winnie's den, smiling and gasping, laughing and calling to one another. "Look!" they cried. "Come look at Winnie!"

They were brave enough to smile. The giggly twin boys who made monkey faces at your Bear; the American soldier whose head was half-covered in bandages blowing her a kiss; the three young women who shouted all of "It's a Long Way to Tipperary" as loud as they could across the moat so they could watch Winnie bounce as she walked.

She had guests to see her in her den nearly every day,

although the variety of treats dwindled. No more scones or custard tarts or golden syrup. It became against the law in England for bakers to even sell fresh bread. Everything, it seemed, was being used up by the War.

She developed a new routine. Each morning, Miss Saunders would come through the gate and say, "Do your daily dozen," and Winnie would perform the new exercises Pfeiffer had taught her, which included lying on her back and pumping her legs, standing, and clapping her paws.

By the time she was finished, the crowds had gathered, and she stood ready to do her duty.

The world changed on a drizzly morning when the first scents of another coming winter found Winnie draped across the slopes of her den, pondering whether it wasn't time for lunch.

A bright, round noise in the distance roused her to her feet. She took a step toward her gate, ready to take cover, but then she stopped. It didn't seem like guns or bombs; it had none of that hard edge to it. For some reason, the sound made your Bear think of romping through a summer field of high yellow grass after Mama.

The noise was joined by others like it, and within

moments, church bells were ringing across London, bobbing against one another while your Bear listened in wonder.

And then there was one bell louder and deeper than them all, which felt like it was tolling from inside Winnie's chest.

Ga-dong.

Ga-dong.

Ga-dong.

Ga-dong.

Ga-dong.

Ga-dong.

Ga-dong.

Ga-dong.

Ga-dong.

Ga-dong.

Ga-dong.

Miss Saunders flung open the gate and rushed in. "It's Big Ben, Winnie!" She clapped her hands together as tears sprouted from her eyes. "They're letting it ring for the first time in years. The War is over! The War is over at last!"

November 11, 1918
Armistice is signed. Great celebrations all day.

In the wake of those bells, the air vibrated as if a great storm had just ended. Winnie listened, feeling slightly dizzy as crowds flooded Regent's Park and the streets outside the Zoo, blowing whistles and bugles, shouting and singing.

Two weeks later, Harry stood in her den.

"We won the Great War, Winnie," he said, sounding slightly stunned.

While he was feeding her, she noticed a fresh badge shaped like an acorn on the cuff of his uniform and touched it with her nose.

"They made me a Major," Harry told her, shrugging at the sky. "Nine days after the fighting ended."

Cole stopped me. "What happened to the other guys? Harry's friends?"

"Edgett went on to be chief of the Vancouver Police Department. And Brodie made it through the War too." I hesitated.

"What about Dixon?"

I'd expected this question. But I still wasn't prepared for it.

"Dixon was wounded less than two months before the end of the War. He should have been okay because his wounds weren't that bad. He was on the deck of a French hospital ship, talking to the other patients, and…well, he just collapsed. His heart gave out. Dixon died of a heart attack. He was forty-eight years old."

Cole's eyes flickered, and he pushed his chin into the top of his Bear's head and bunched his blanket in his fingers.

Softly, I said, "It doesn't seem fair, does it?"

Cole closed and opened his brown eyes once, twice, but they stayed clear. "That's because it's not," he said with a grown-up shake of his head.

They sat together on the slopes, Harry petting your Bear calmly, each of them lost in their thoughts.

"In Winnipeg," said Harry, "it's so cold you can feel icicles on the insides of your nose. Have I ever told you that? You're much too big to sleep under the bed now, so I guess—"

Someone called to them from across the empty moat. "Winnie," boomed Pfeiffer, "who's that with you? Is that your soldier?"

Winnie stood on her hind legs beside Harry.

Pfeiffer took off his hat to reveal his thin gray hair sticking straight up. "Thank you, good sir! Thank you for bringing us Winnie, our favorite bear!" He glanced into the next den and cleared his throat. "Forgive me, Sam. I meant our favorite *black bear*, *Ursus americanus*. Polar bears, *Ursus maritimus*, are an entirely different subspecies."

Someone whistled from the walkway that overlooked the back of her den, and Winnie went to see who it was. A boy in a brown cap tossed her an apple, and she leapt and caught it in her mouth.

Winnie wagged her head. "Thanks, Charlie!"

Harry laughed. "You've made quite a life for yourself here, haven't you?" he said, ruffling the fur on top of her head as she settled beside him to eat. Harry sighed in a satisfied way. "All I wanted, ever since I found you in White River, was for you to be loved. And look," he said, lifting his hand to wave back at the spectators now waving at them. "Look at how loved you are."

Winnie rested her chin on his knee.

"I won't take it personally," he said. "After all, it's not much of a choice between living in the world's finest zoo and living in a freezing-cold stall with no one to talk to but me and a sick donkey."

The sun set, and the Zoo closed, but Miss Saunders said Harry could stay as long as he wanted. He lay on his back on the slopes, looking at the stars, with your Bear's head on his chest, listening to his heart.

Sam was snoring next door.

"I have to let you go, Winnie," Harry said very quietly. "The War taught me about sacrifice, if nothing else. I've seen so many people give up what's dearest to them, all for something greater."

He kissed the top of her head. "You will always be my Bear." His fingers found the special place at the back of her neck, and her eyes began to close, and his heartbeat sounded like Mama's.

When she woke up, he was gone.

Cole fidgeted with his Bear's ear. "I would never have left her."

"You wouldn't have?" I said. "But then what happened next could never have happened. Something even greater than the Great War was waiting for your Bear. And if it wasn't for that, this story might have never been remembered and told."

Some years after the War, a four-year-old boy and his father were led through the tunnels inside the Terraces and up the steep wooden steps to Winnie's den. The boy wore an itchy coat that ended just above his knees; his unusually long, wavy hair covered his ears. He had a dimple in the middle of his chin, just like Harry.

The boy held back, clutching his father's leg. "It's all right," said Zookeeper Graves, who had returned to his position after the War. "She won't harm you."

Winnie approached slowly and opened her mouth. "Who are you?" she wanted to know.

She'd been visited by children before, but there was something special about this one. She could smell it.

"My name is Christopher Robin Milne." His father bent to murmur in his ear, and the boy pulled a very small stuffed animal from his coat. He showed it to your Bear. It had three buttons down its front and a tiny snout and ears that were too big, and it held its paws in the air in a very excitable way. "And this is Piglet," said the boy. "Say hello, Piglet."

Winnie was surprised to find that Piglet smelled like the Woods.

The boy glanced at the pond at the front of her den. "Would you like to join us on an Expotition? Piglet wants to cross the sea, except she might be scared."

Not two moments later, Christopher Robin and Piglet were riding on Winnie's back through the puddle. "Don't drop us! Hold steady! Watch out for the waves! What's that up ahead? Go on, silly bear, go on!"

Christopher Robin came back again and again. He named his teddy bear after Winnie. From the walkway above the den, his father, Mr. Milne, watched their adventures with delight. Sometimes he'd write in a small notebook and chuckle.

When Christopher Robin was six years old, Mr. Milne wrote *Winnie-the-Pooh*, which was an overnight success. Then he wrote *The House at Pooh Corner*.

That's how Winnie became Christopher Robin's bear.

So many have felt the same way about your Bear. Her Mama, of course. And the trapper's boy. The men of the Second Canadian Infantry Brigade. And everyone at the Zoo.

Harry.

Christopher Robin.

Me.

And you.

Most amazing of all, the whole world too.

That's the entire story, the real one, the true story of Winnie, who was brave enough to go Farther Than Any Bear Has Ever Gone, all the way through a century to come back in this story for you.

Cole got up and carried his Bear by one leg over to the shelf next to his closet, which was crammed with treasures: a wooden lighthouse from our trip to Tobermory, a photo of him and his friend Asher atop Huckleberry Rock, his bronze ski medal, the space-age crystal-growing kit he'd won at the fall fair.

He reached to the back for my worn copy of The House at Pooh Corner, the one my grandfather gave me, and stood the book up at the shelf's edge, propping its front cover open with his stuffed animal. A creased black-and-white photo was taped inside. It was of Cole's great-great-grandfather, the courageous man he had been named for. He was holding a little something out for Bear, who stood up straight and held Harry's wrist tenderly with one paw, eager to taste whatever came next.

And my Boy saluted them both.

The Colebourn Family Archive

My great-grandfather Harry Colebourn opened his diary on August 24, 1914, and recorded the purchase of a small black bear cub for twenty dollars. At that time, he couldn't possibly have imagined that the events that would follow would eventually help inspire one of the most beloved children's stories of all time. Growing up with this incredible family story instilled in me a lasting notion that the world was a very big place that could be shaped in part by the smallest of loving gestures.

The story of Harry and Winnie, set against the backdrop of the events of the Great War, reminds us of how much had to be lost for so much to be gained. It is this legacy of love and kindness, as well as bravery and sacrifice, that I am grateful to share with my own children, Cole and Claudia, and with readers everywhere.

In addition to his 1914 diary, Harry left behind

other items that make up our family archive. The photographs, artifacts, and additional diaries that anchor the events of *Winnie's Great War* in world history have captured my imagination for as long as I can remember. They have also served to make the somewhat surreal story of a soldier bringing a bear cub to war that would go on to inspire a very famous literary character seem all the more real to me. On the following pages you will find some of the most treasured items from our family archive. I hope they serve as a reminder that sometimes the best stories are, in fact, true.

Lindsay Mattick

Here is a photograph of Harry as a young soldier. Harry was born in Birmingham, England, on April 12, 1887, the second eldest of six children. When he was young, his father took a position as a groomsman on a rural estate, where he was responsible for the carriages, stables, and care of the horses. This experience likely helped foster a deep, and fateful, love of animals in Harry. Harry went on to become a trained veterinarian and was already a military volunteer working with animals when the Great War broke out in the summer of 1914.

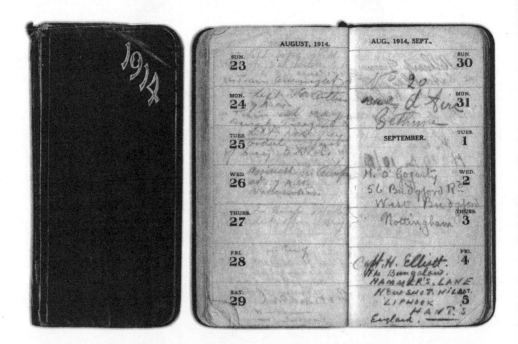

Monday, August 24, 1914: *Left Pt. Arthur 7 AM. On train all day. Bought Bear $20.* This entry in Harry's diary marks the beginning of Harry and Winnie's journey together. The diaries that Harry kept between 1914 and 1918 leave a personal account of his experiences through the Great War.

I have always loved this particular photograph of Harry feeding Winnie, as it captures such a tender moment. The inscription on the back of this photograph reads: *Yours very sincerely, myself and Winnie the Bear. Winnie is now on Exhibition at the Zoo in London but is coming back with me someday. Kind Regards to all. Arry.* As we now know, Harry donated Winnie to the London Zoo on December 1, 1919, after the Great War had ended.

This photograph of Harry and Winnie inspired sculptor Bill Epp's statues that now stand in Winnipeg and London. The back of the photograph is inscribed with a note from Harry: *Have had a head shave as you will see by picture—what do you think of my new pal. H.C.* My grandfather Fred Colebourn, Harry's only son, was determined to have his father's story commemorated. It was his considerable efforts that led to the creation of these statues.

Winnie is pictured here with the Winnipeg section of the Canadian Army Veterinary Corps; the photograph was taken in Valcartier, Quebec, where the Canadian soldiers trained before departing for Europe. Harry is in the second row, the second soldier from the left. We know the names of some of the other soldiers in this photo too: Brodie is in the first row, seated fourth from the left; Edgett is in the middle row, second from the right.

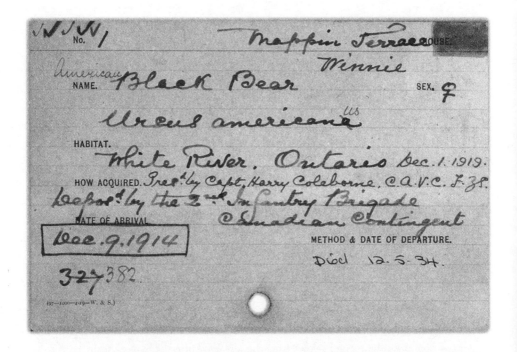

The handwritten animal record card reads:

No. 1

Mappin Terrace House

Winnie

NAME. American Black Bear   SEX. ♀

Ursus americanus

HABITAT. White River. Ontario   Dec. 1. 1919.

HOW ACQUIRED. Pres^d by Capt. Harry Coleborne, C.A.V.C. F.35.
Deposd by the 2nd Infantry Brigade
Canadian Contingent

DATE OF ARRIVAL
Dec. 9. 1914

METHOD & DATE OF DEPARTURE.
Died 12. 5. 34.

327 382

(97—1000—4·19—W. & S.)

*This animal record card shows us that Harry first brought Winnie to the London Zoo on December 9, 1914. In the year and a half following Winnie's arrival at the zoo, five other black bears, also Canadian regimental mascots, were donated to the zoo. Winnie's home was the newly constructed Mappin Terraces, named for its benefactor, the jewelry and cutlery company Mappin & Webb.

This photograph, taken in 1925, shows Christopher Robin playing with Winnie as his father, A. A. Milne, watches from above. Winnie was considered a star attraction at the London Zoo, where she lived for more than twenty years.

This photograph was taken of Harry standing outside the veterinary clinic that he established in Winnipeg following the war. Also pictured is his veterinarian kit with some of the instruments he used in his practice. Harry was known in the community for caring for the animals he loved even when their owners could not afford to pay for his services.

Our family tree comes full circle, as my son's name is short for Colebourn. Cole, named after his great-grandfather, is pictured here with me. He is five years old and just beginning to understand his good fortune to have a "great-great-grandbear."

"Did that really happen?" asked Cole.

This is a work of imagination rooted in historical fact. We know very little about Winnie's story before Harry bought her from the trapper in White River, and what we do know of her life comes almost entirely from Harry's brief diary entries, Colebourn family stories, and zoo records and newspaper articles from that time. Details about the Great War, including Valcartier, Salisbury Plain, and life in London during the war years, are based on research. Brodie, Dixon, and Edgett were real members of the Canadian Army Veterinary Corps, and the fates of Dixon and Edgett are true; but we imagined Harry's relationships with them and what they might have been like. There really was a stampede at Valcartier and zeppelin attacks over London. Sergeant Bill was real. So were Sam and Barbara, the polar bears who were Winnie's neighbors on the Mappin Terraces; Sam really did like to steal people's umbrellas. The characters

Winnie meets at the zoo are inspired by real people who worked at or visited the zoo, but again, Winnie's relationships with them came from our own imaginations. We do know, however, about one very special guest: Christopher Robin Milne.